HAUNTED TREASURE HUNT

A Halloween Inspired Coloring Book

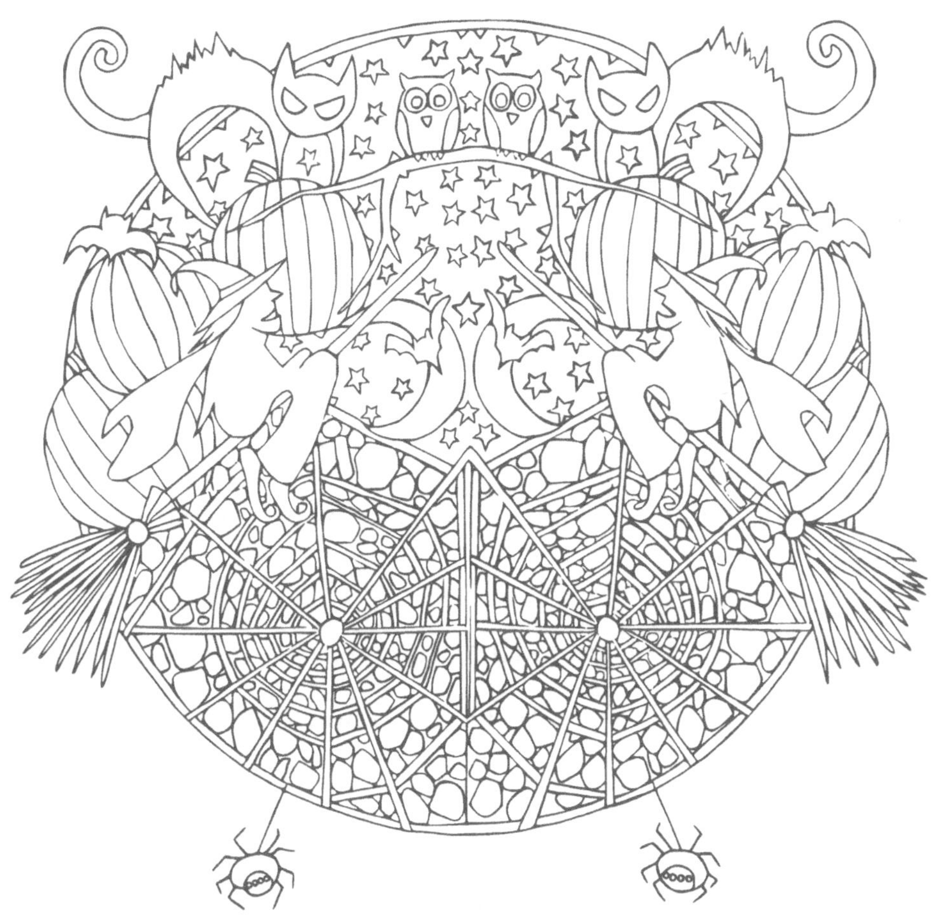

Featuring the artwork of:

Julia Abby Thomas

Toy Surge Press is an imprint of Toy Surge Group

For more information visit: www.ToySurgeBooks.com

Haunted Treasure Hunt

A Halloween Inspired Coloring Book

International Standard Book Number

ISBN-13: 978-0-9903814-1-9

ISBN-10: 0-9903814-1-2

FIRST EDITION

INTRODUCTION

Welcome to my inky haunted world!

This Halloween a spell has been placed upon you. You wake one night to find yourself in a mysterious and dark world. You must find the good witch for help to bring you back home but you need to collect all the key ingredients she needs to destroy the spell.

You can skip around but don't get lost. The path was made to be followed. One slight misstep and you can be lost here forever!

Inside this book, you'll find fun black and white Halloween themed illustrations. There are pictures to color, mazes to solve and illustrations to complete where you can create your own doodles and details.

Use the Haunted Treasure Hunt List to help you keep track of all the things you find and need to collect.

Good luck!

Tip! Mandalas and mazes do not contain any key ingredients the good witch needs. Colored pencils are best for color blending in this coloring book. If using any water-based ink pens, place a sheet of paper or thin cardboard under the page for best results to prevent any possible bleed through.

Haunted Treasure Hunt List

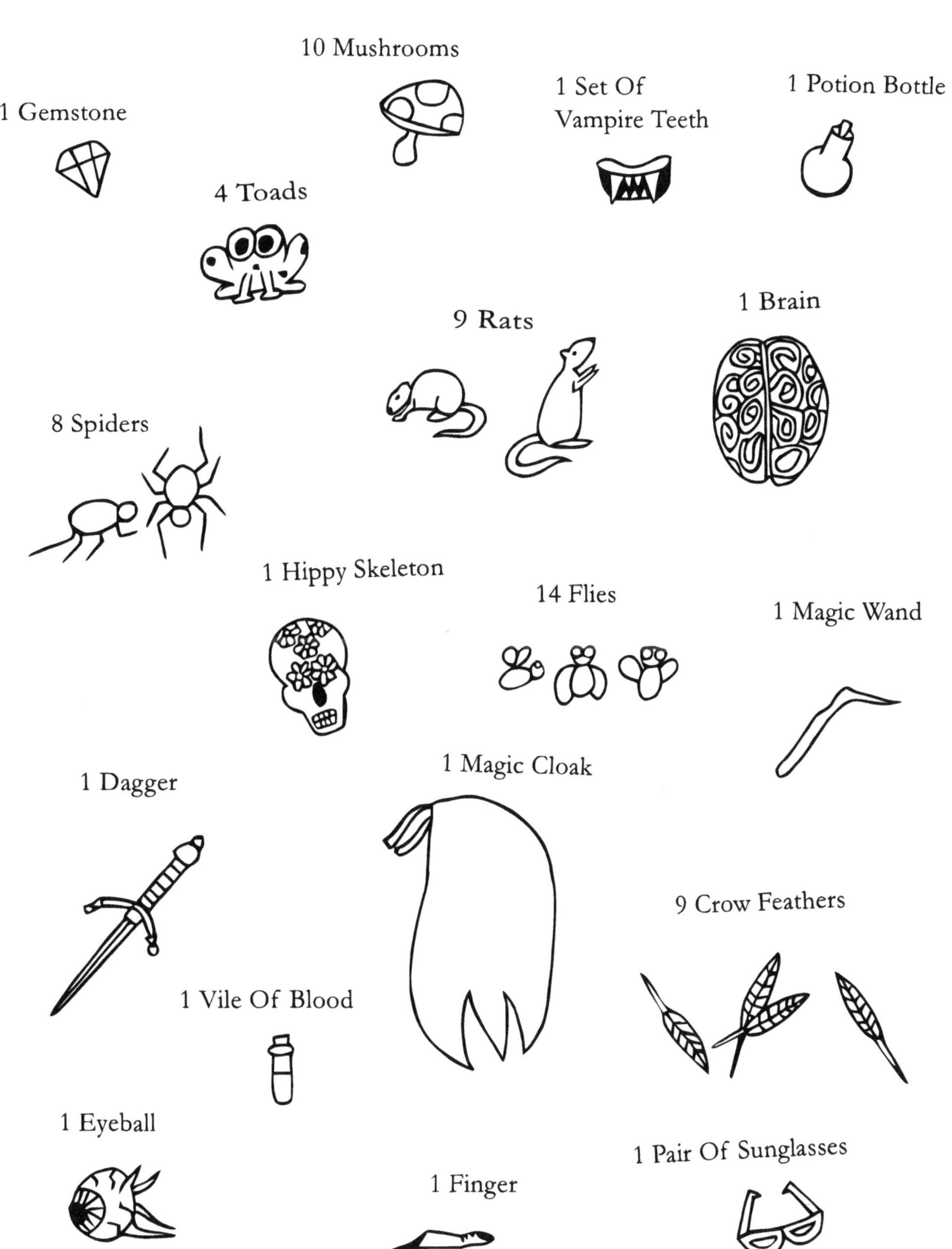

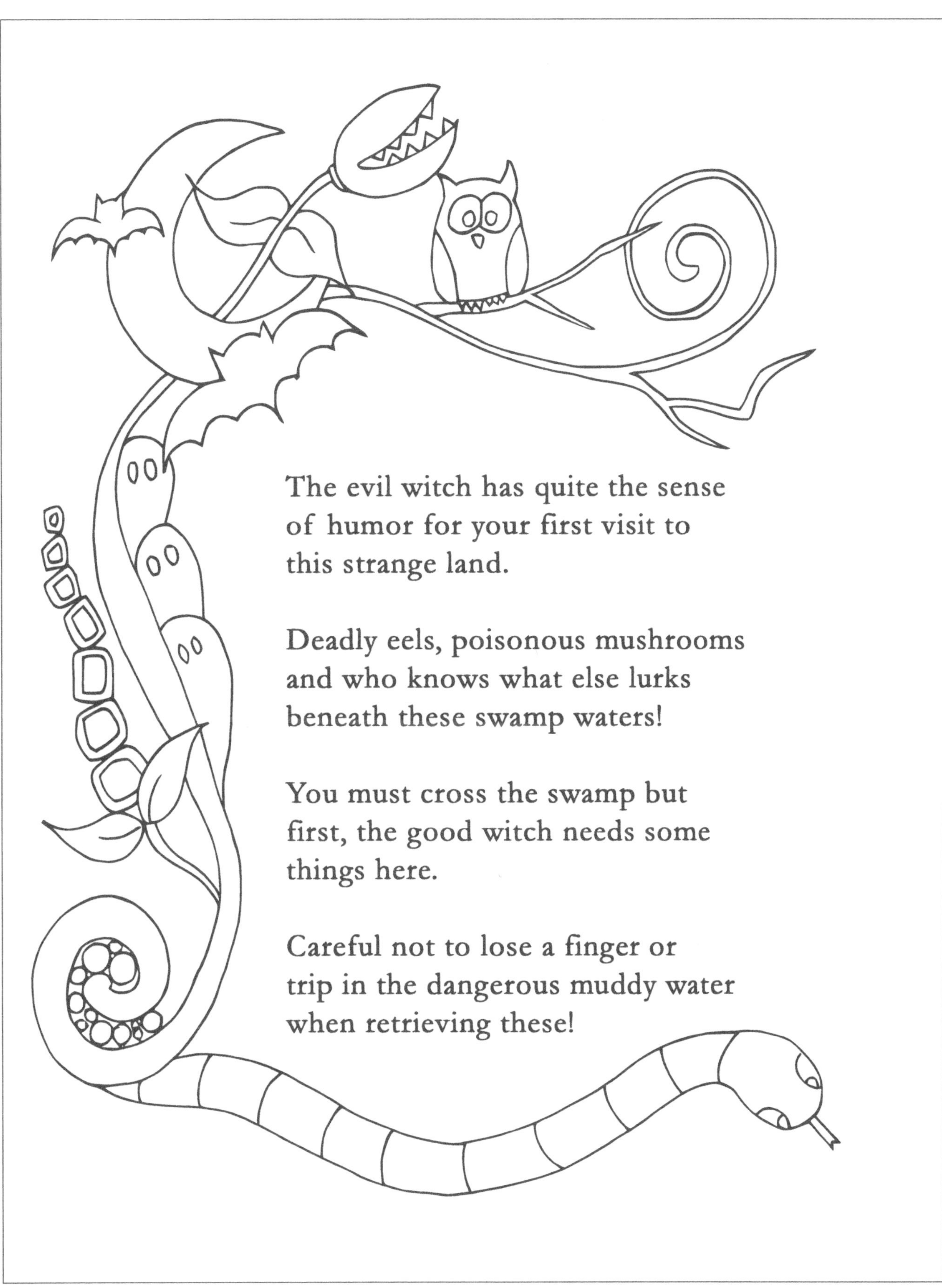

The evil witch has quite the sense
of humor for your first visit to
this strange land.

Deadly eels, poisonous mushrooms
and who knows what else lurks
beneath these swamp waters!

You must cross the swamp but
first, the good witch needs some
things here.

Careful not to lose a finger or
trip in the dangerous muddy water
when retrieving these!

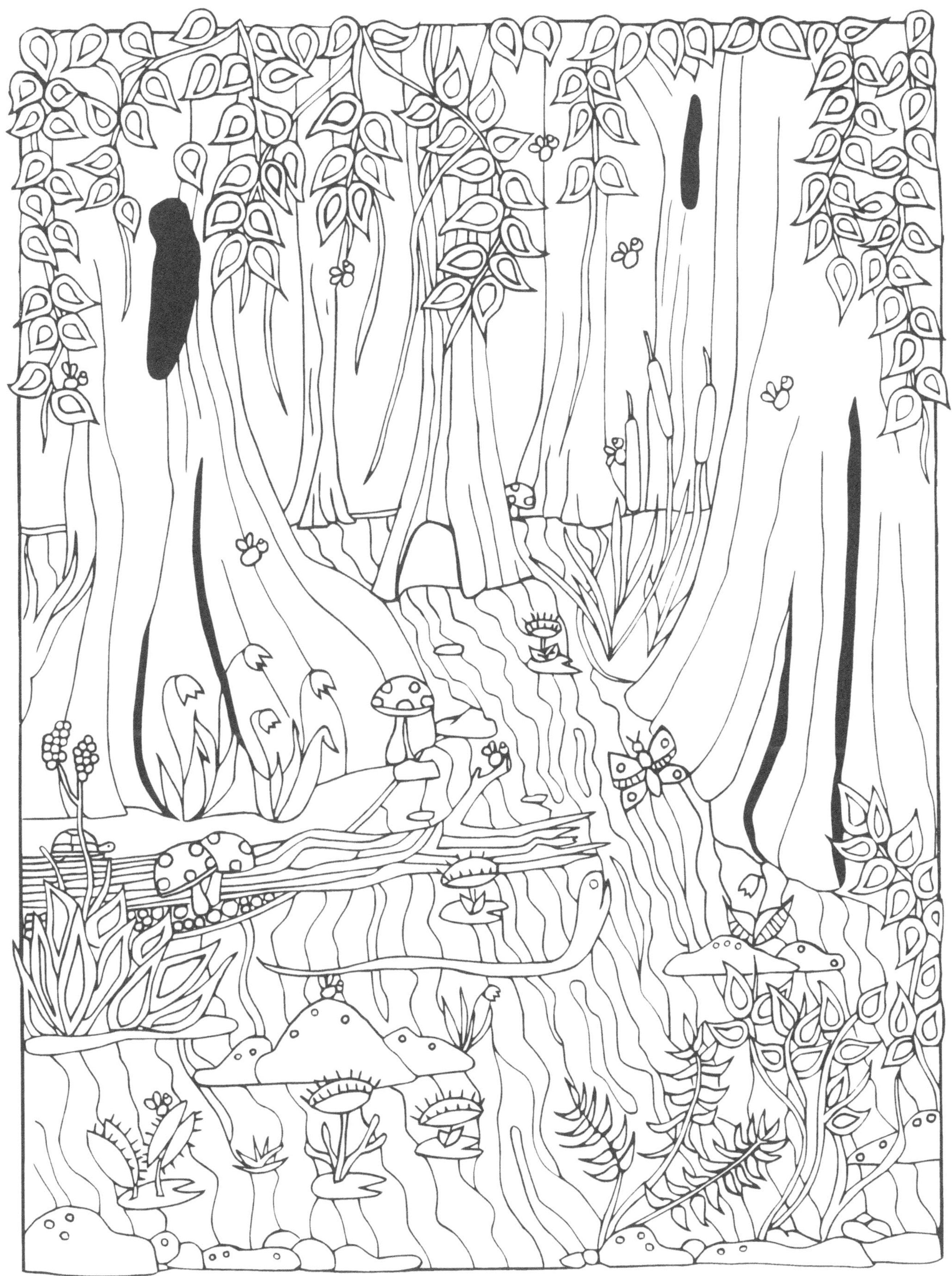

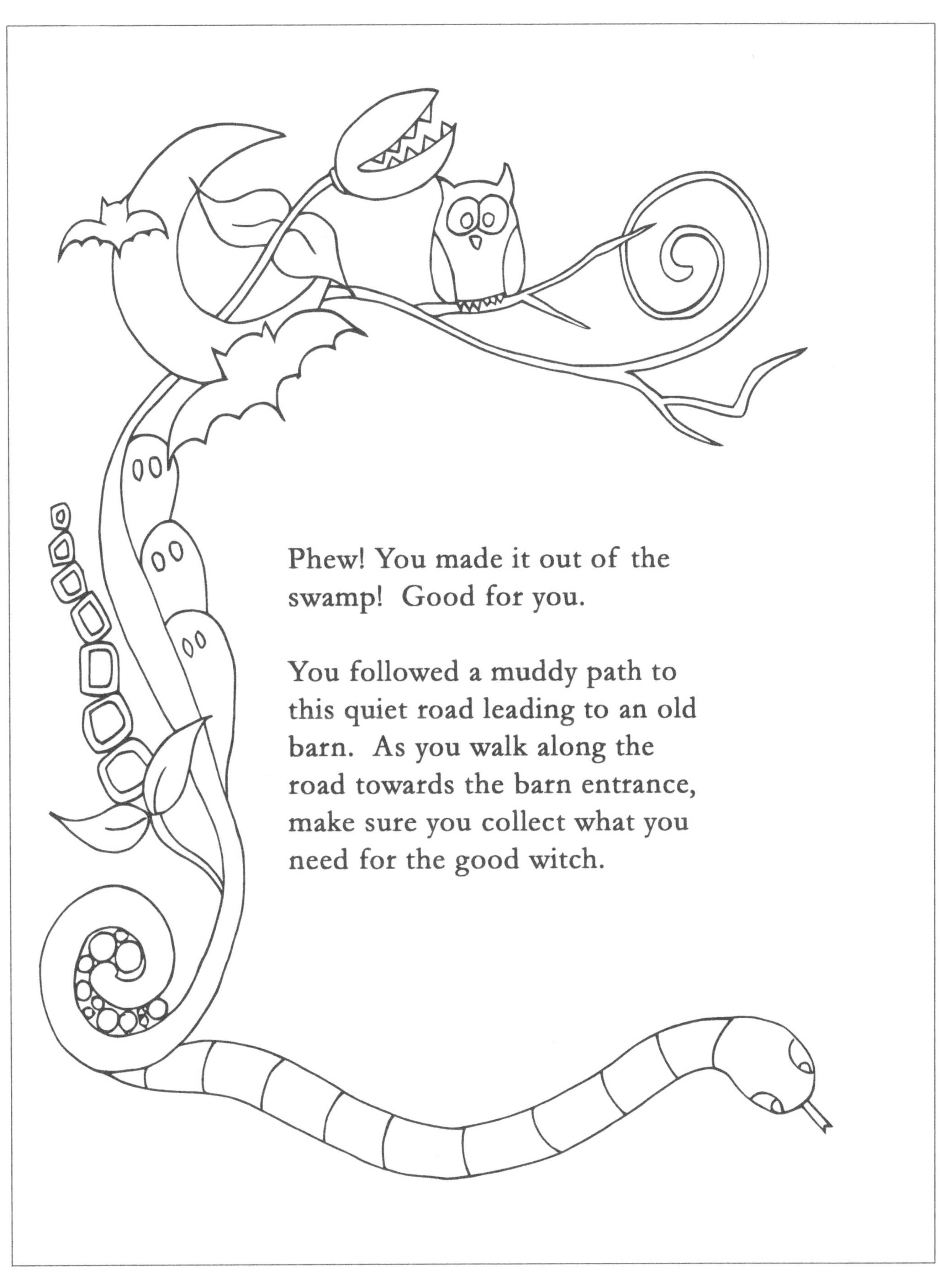

Phew! You made it out of the swamp! Good for you.

You followed a muddy path to this quiet road leading to an old barn. As you walk along the road towards the barn entrance, make sure you collect what you need for the good witch.

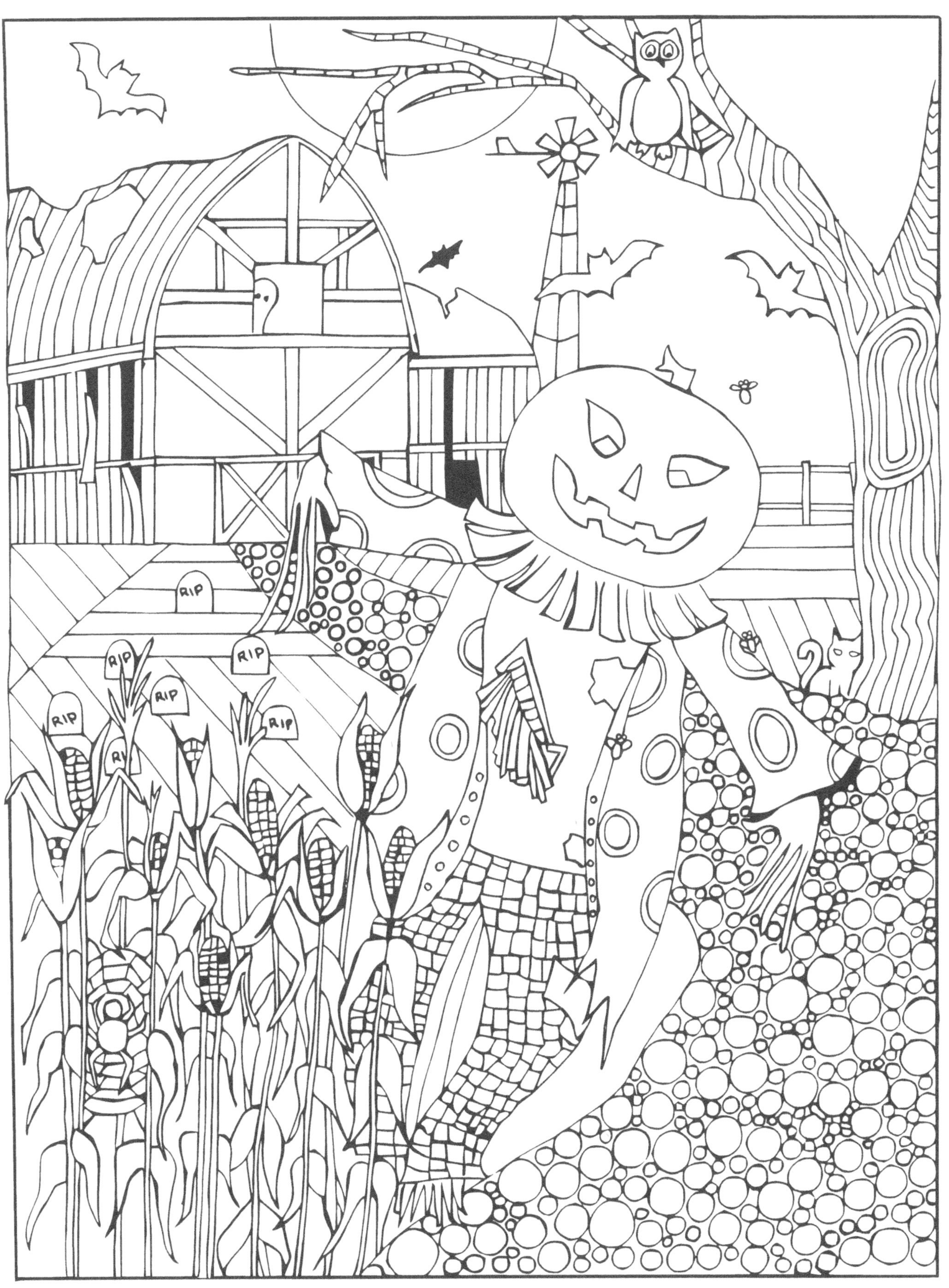
RIP
RIP
RIP
RIP
RIP
RIP

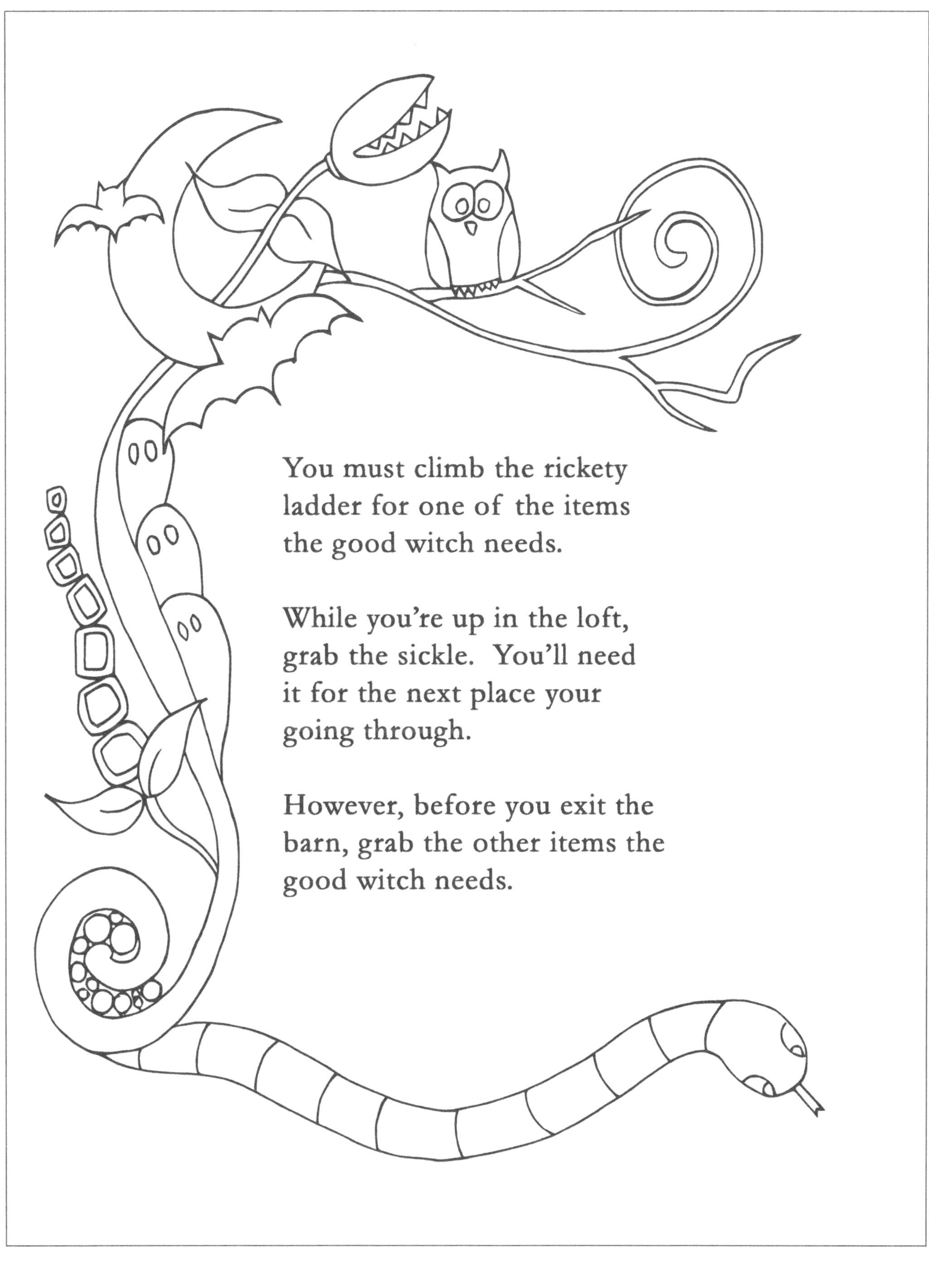

You must climb the rickety ladder for one of the items the good witch needs.

While you're up in the loft, grab the sickle. You'll need it for the next place your going through.

However, before you exit the barn, grab the other items the good witch needs.

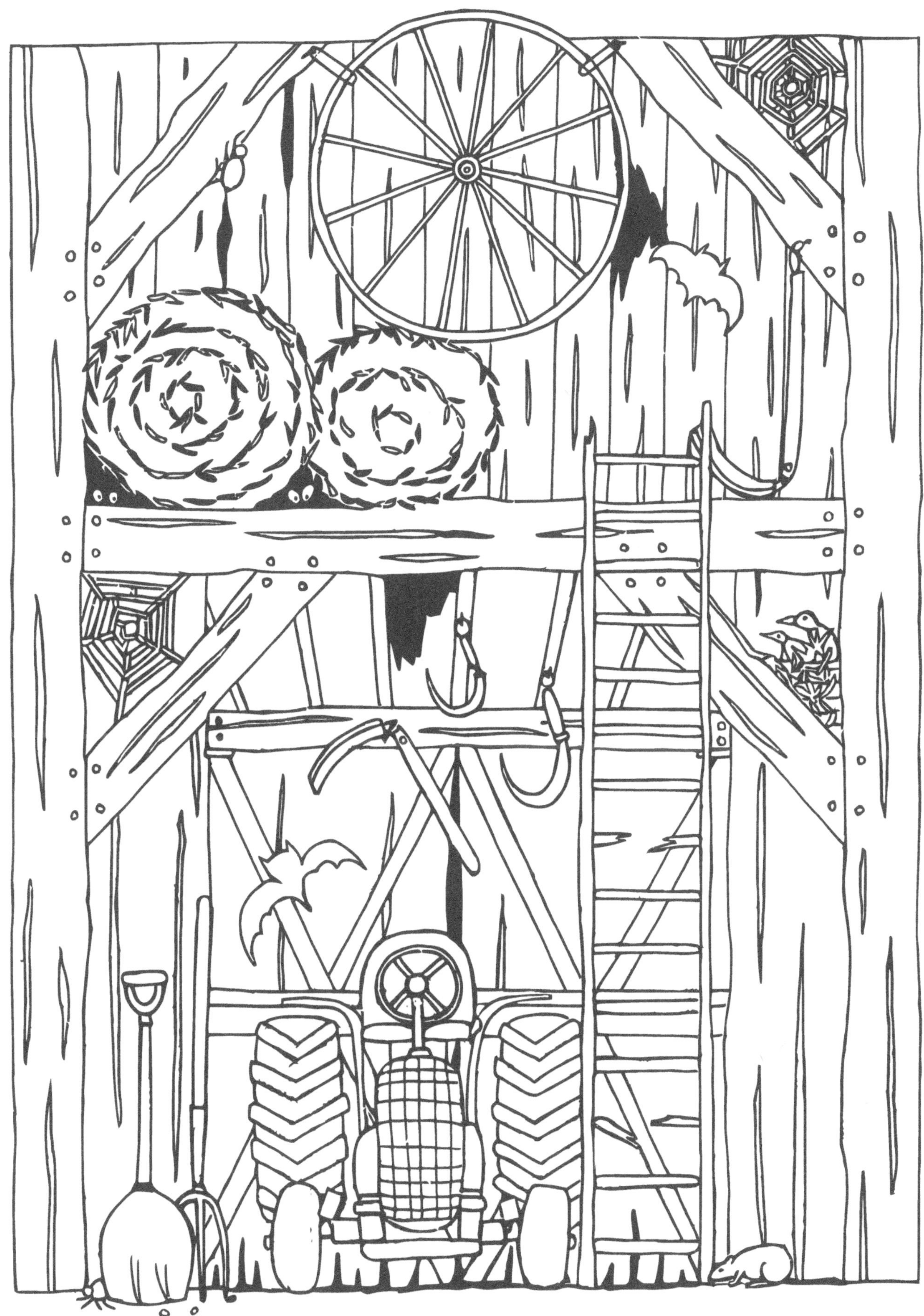

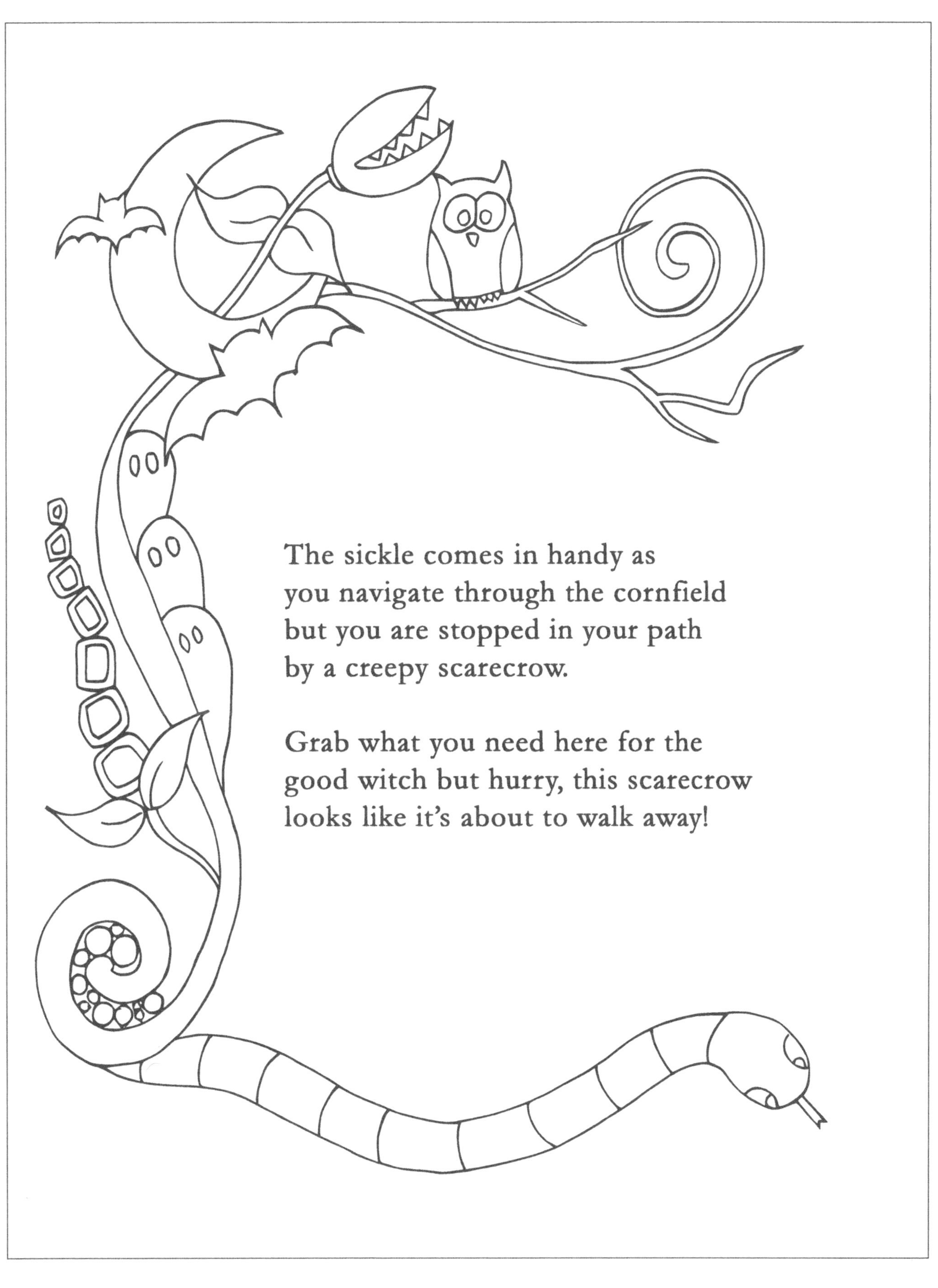

The sickle comes in handy as
you navigate through the cornfield
but you are stopped in your path
by a creepy scarecrow.

Grab what you need here for the
good witch but hurry, this scarecrow
looks like it's about to walk away!

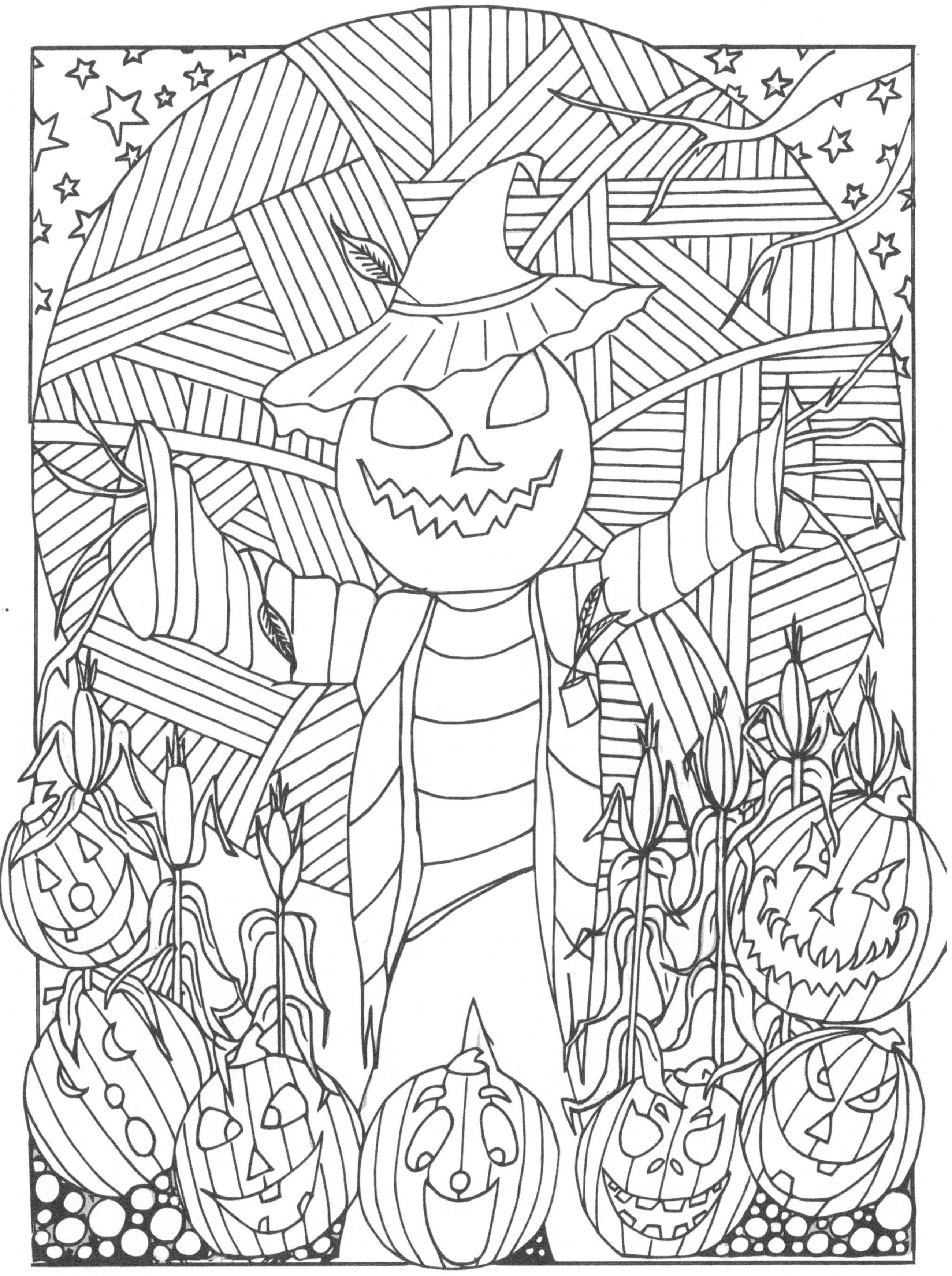

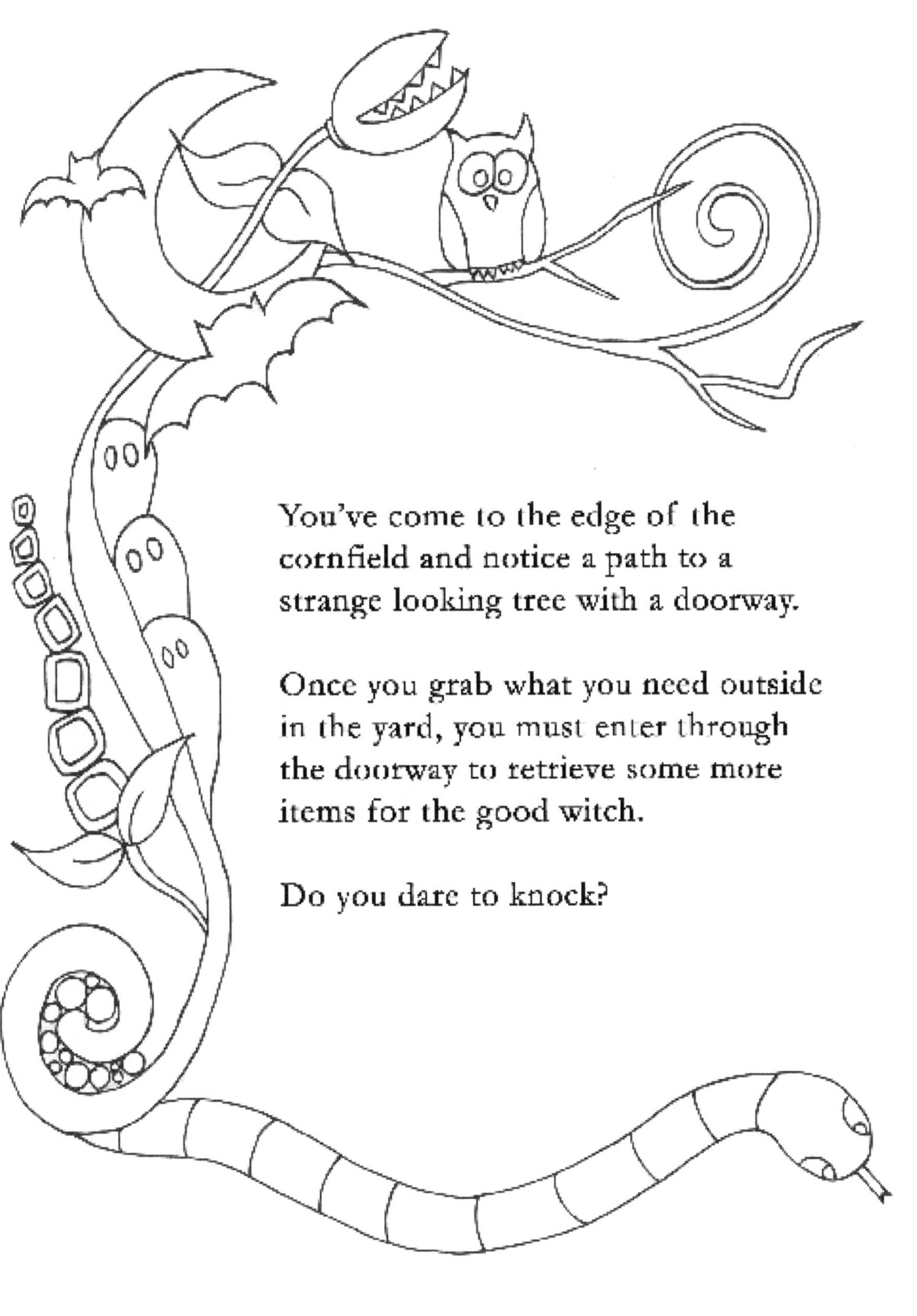

You've come to the edge of the cornfield and notice a path to a strange looking tree with a doorway.

Once you grab what you need outside in the yard, you must enter through the doorway to retrieve some more items for the good witch.

Do you dare to knock?

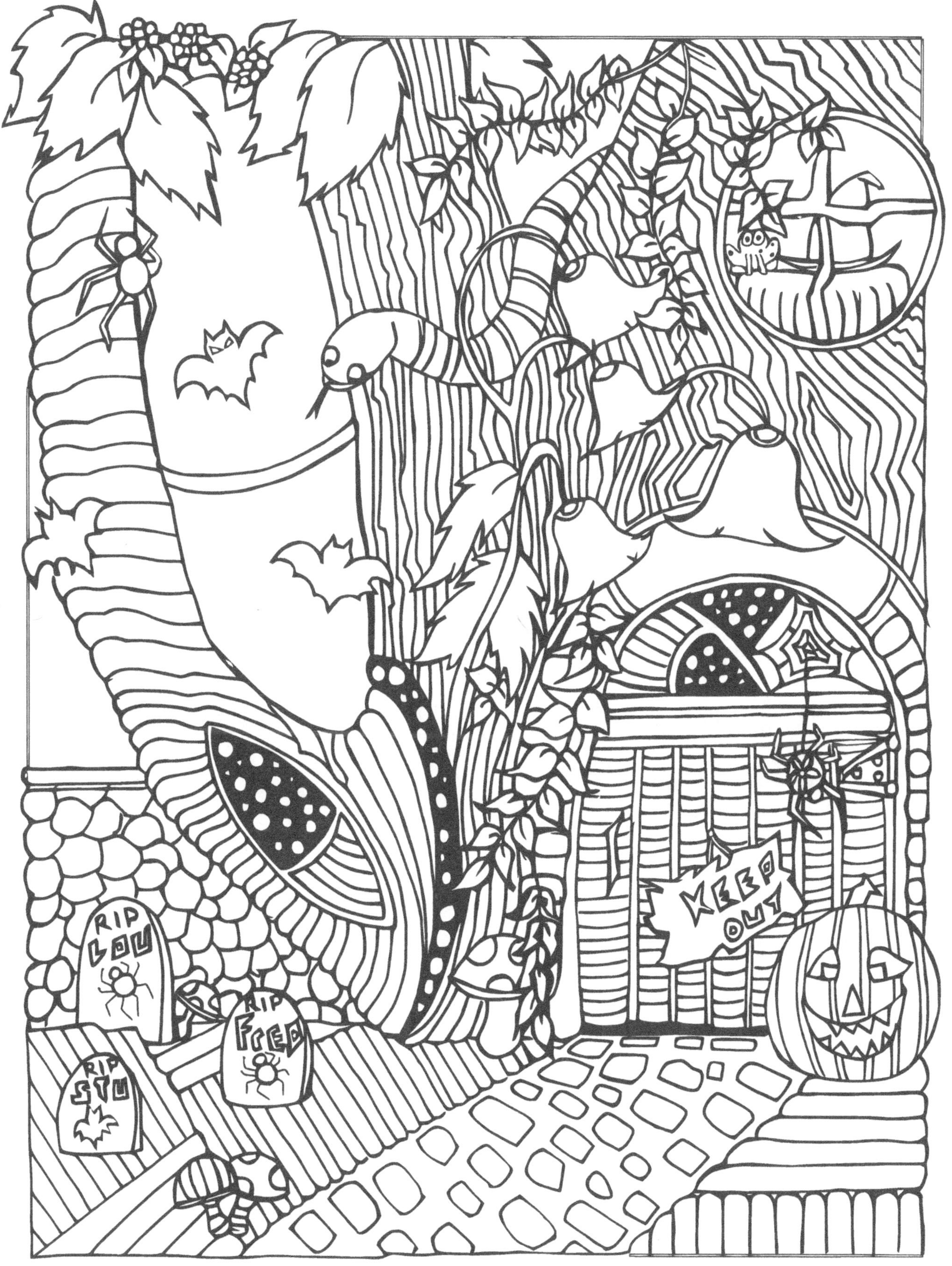
RIP
LOU
RIP
FRED
RIP
STU
KEEP
OUT

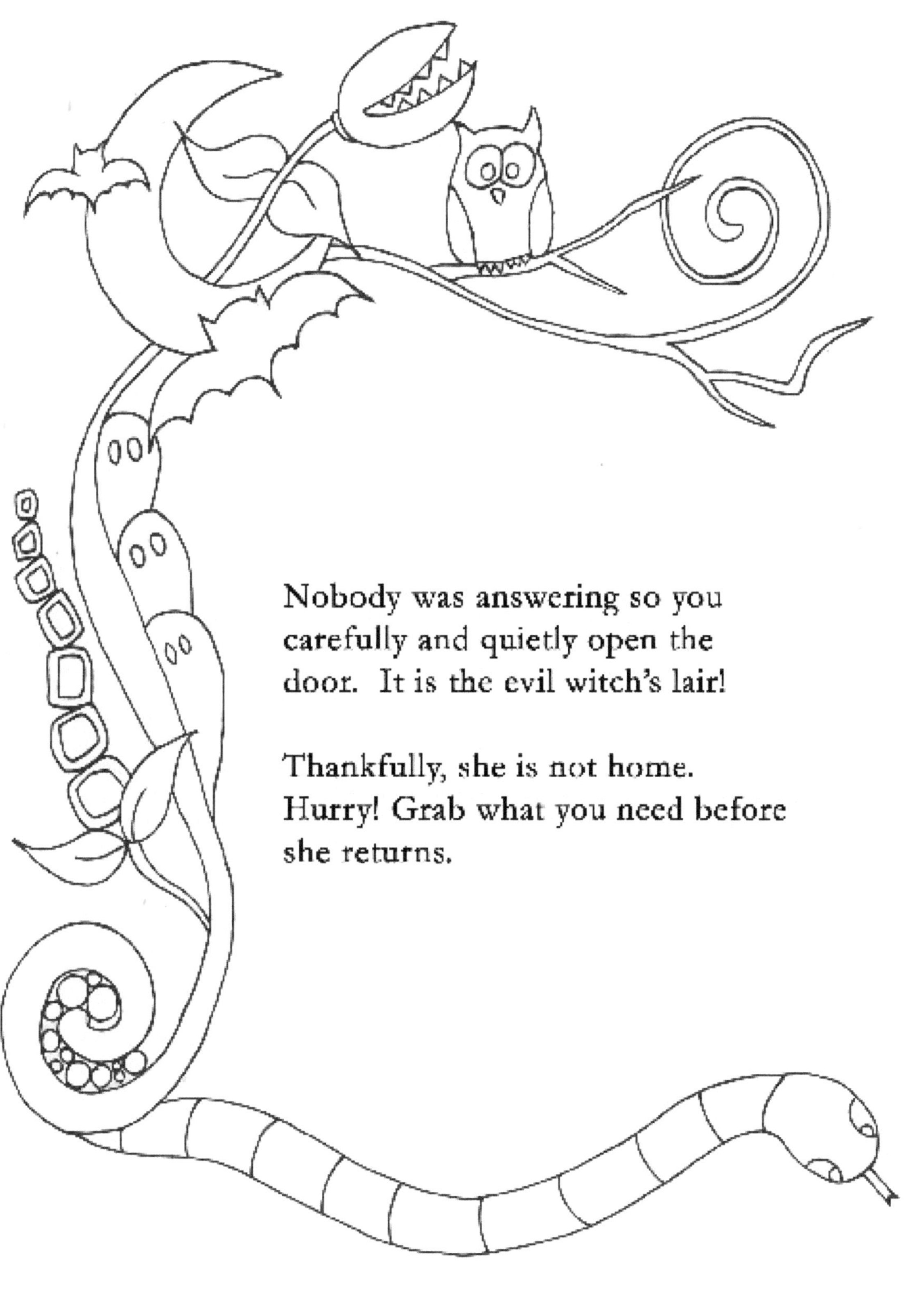

Nobody was answering so you carefully and quietly open the door. It is the evil witch's lair!

Thankfully, she is not home. Hurry! Grab what you need before she returns.

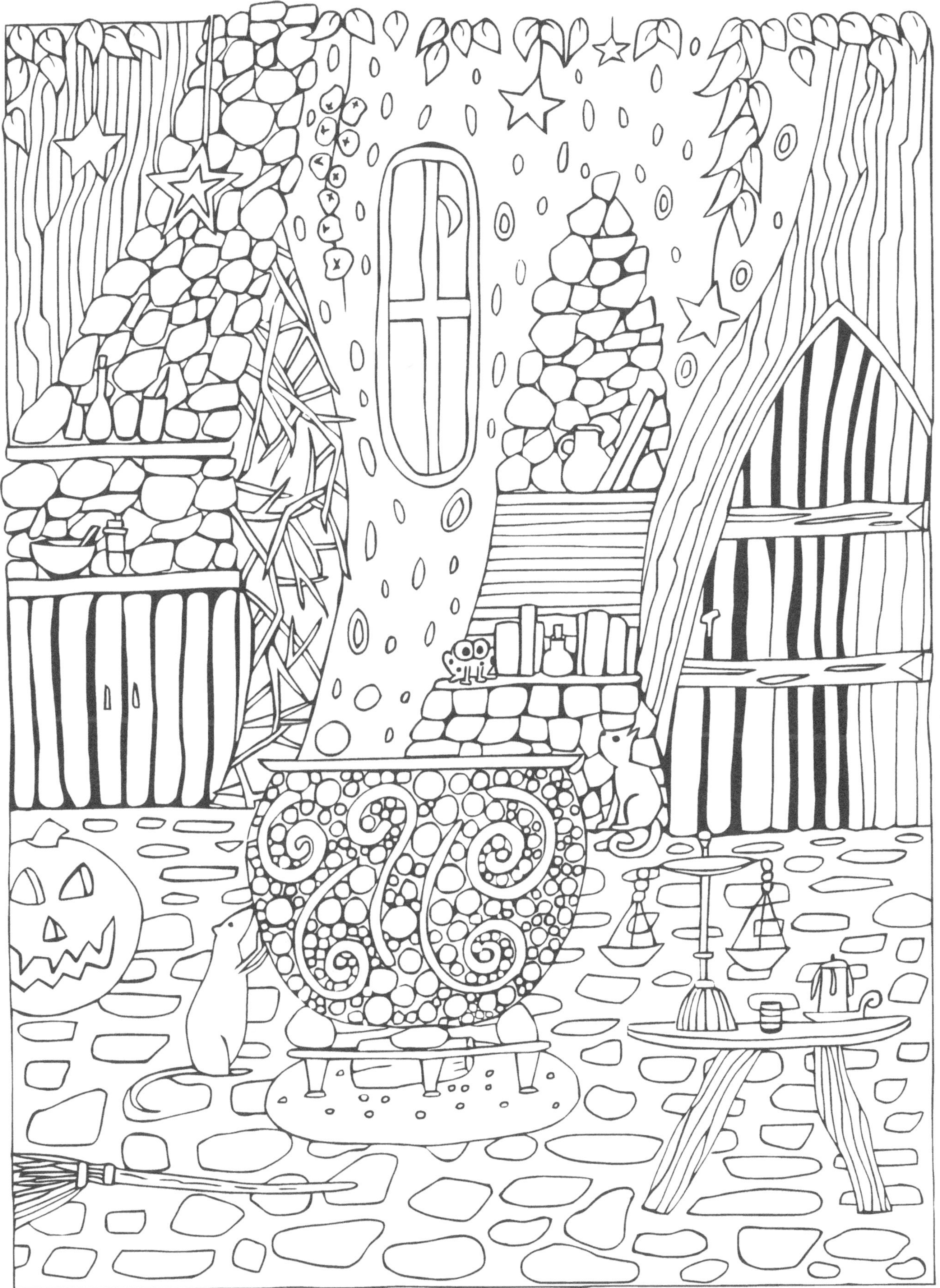

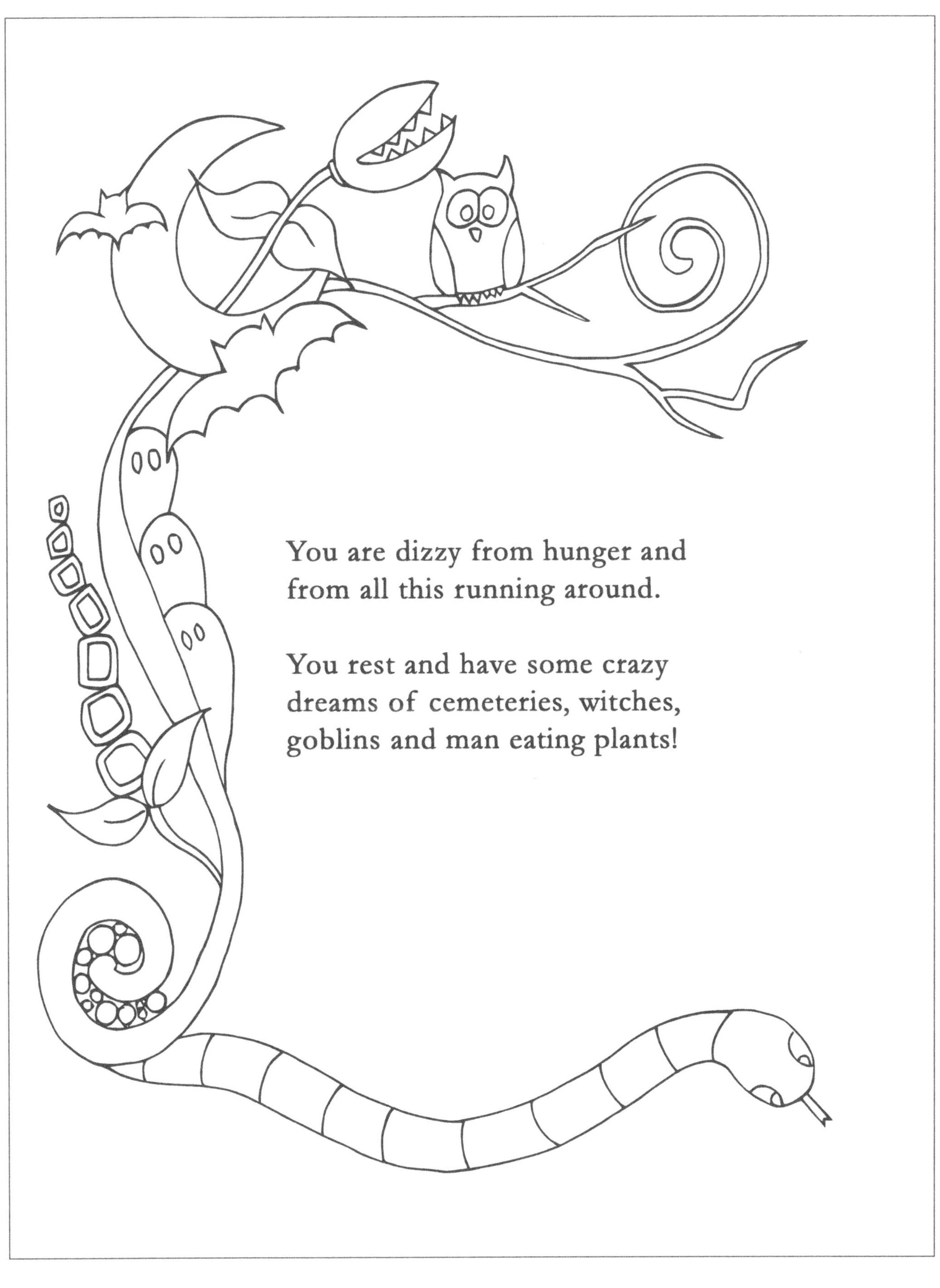

You are dizzy from hunger and from all this running around.

You rest and have some crazy dreams of cemeteries, witches, goblins and man eating plants!

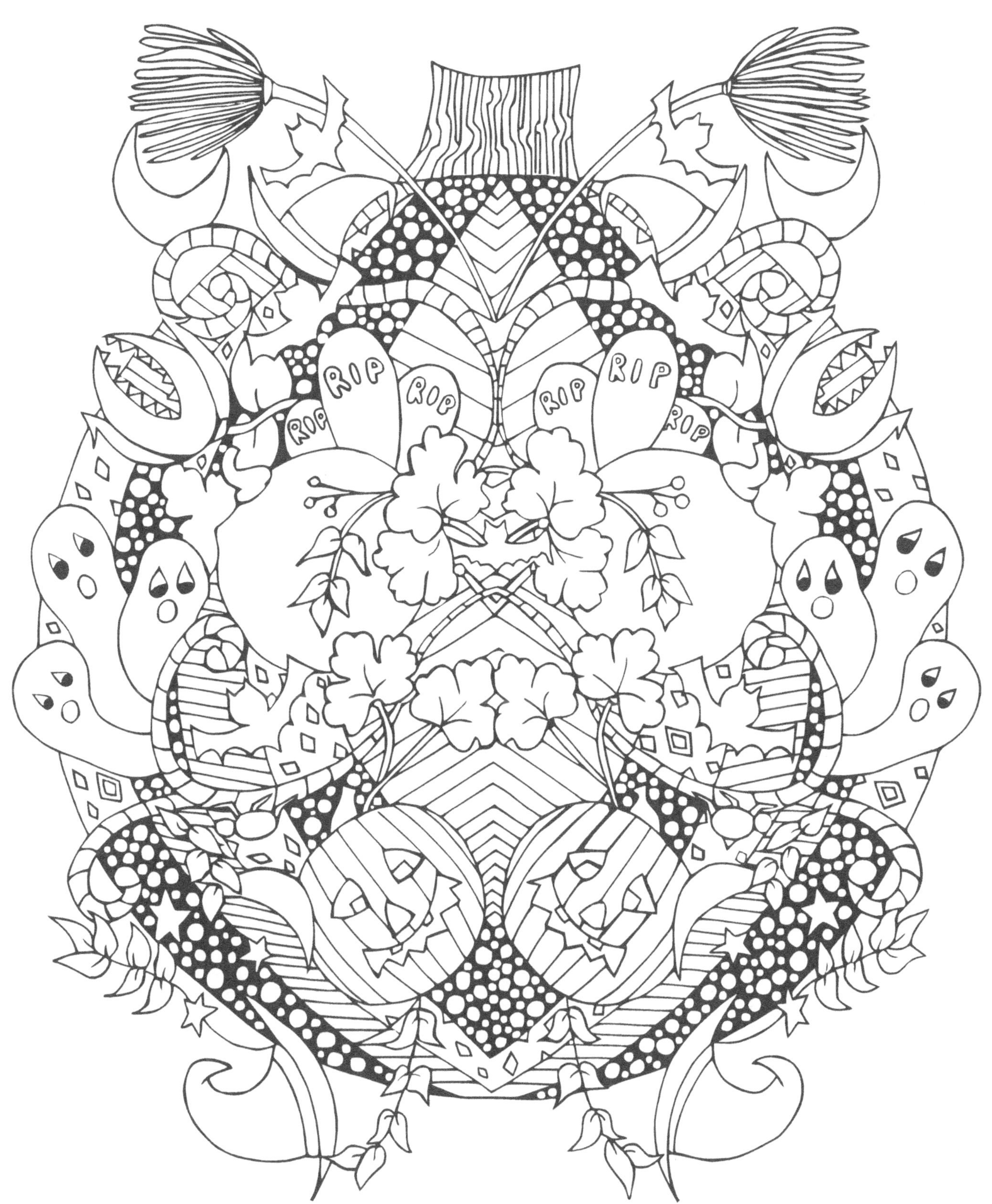
RIP
RIP
RIP
RIP
RIP
RIP

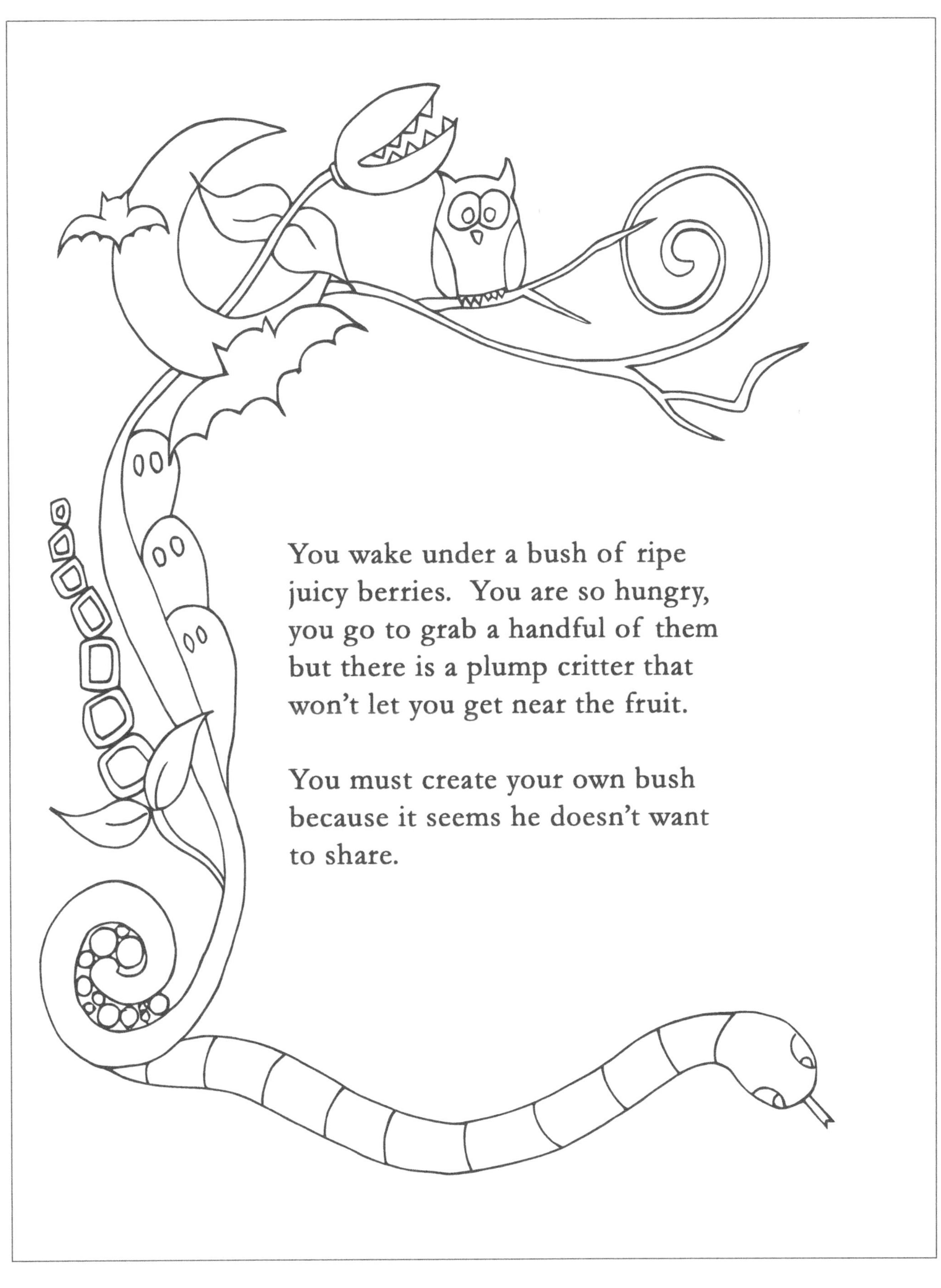

You wake under a bush of ripe juicy berries. You are so hungry, you go to grab a handful of them but there is a plump critter that won't let you get near the fruit.

You must create your own bush because it seems he doesn't want to share.

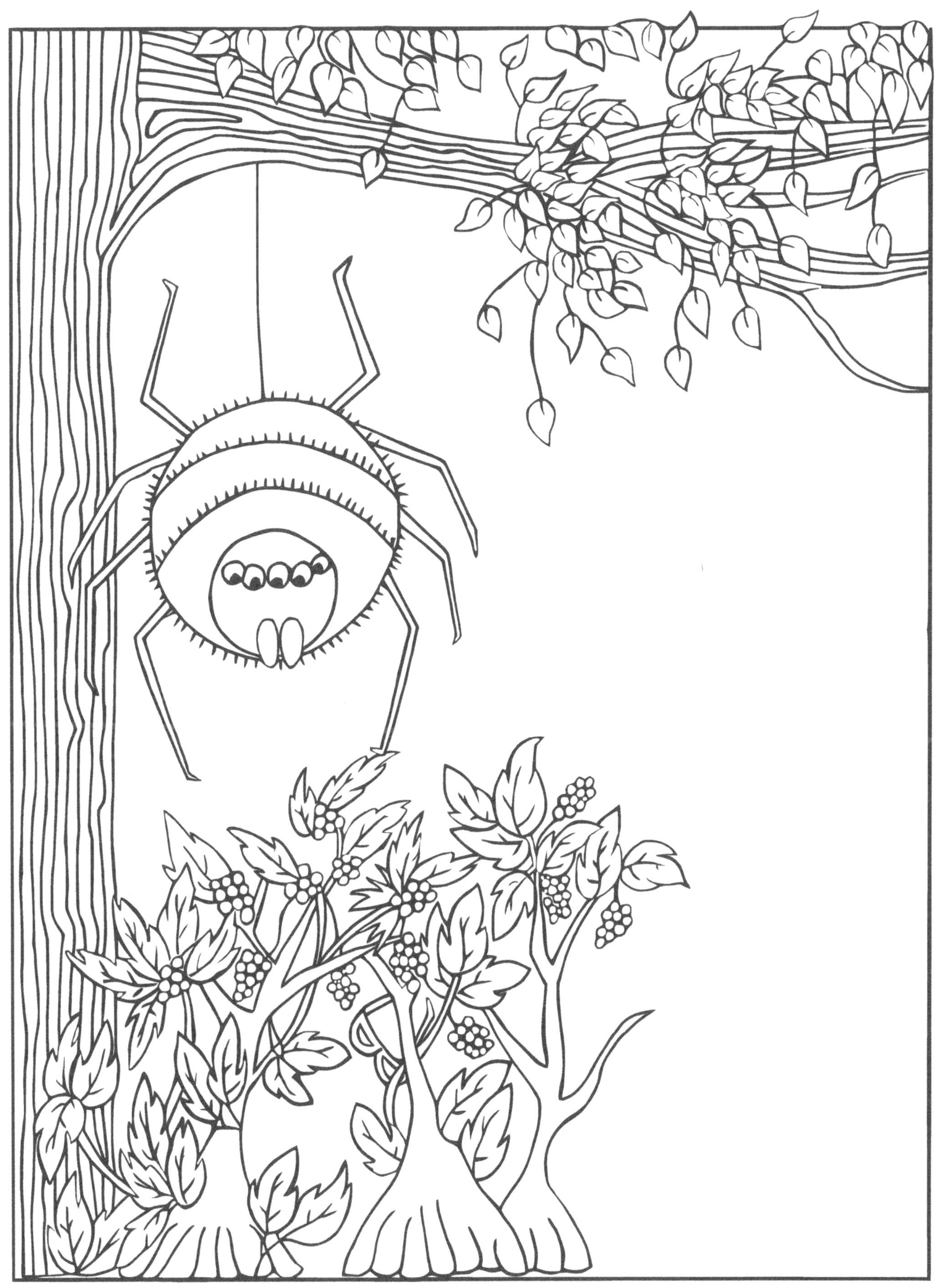

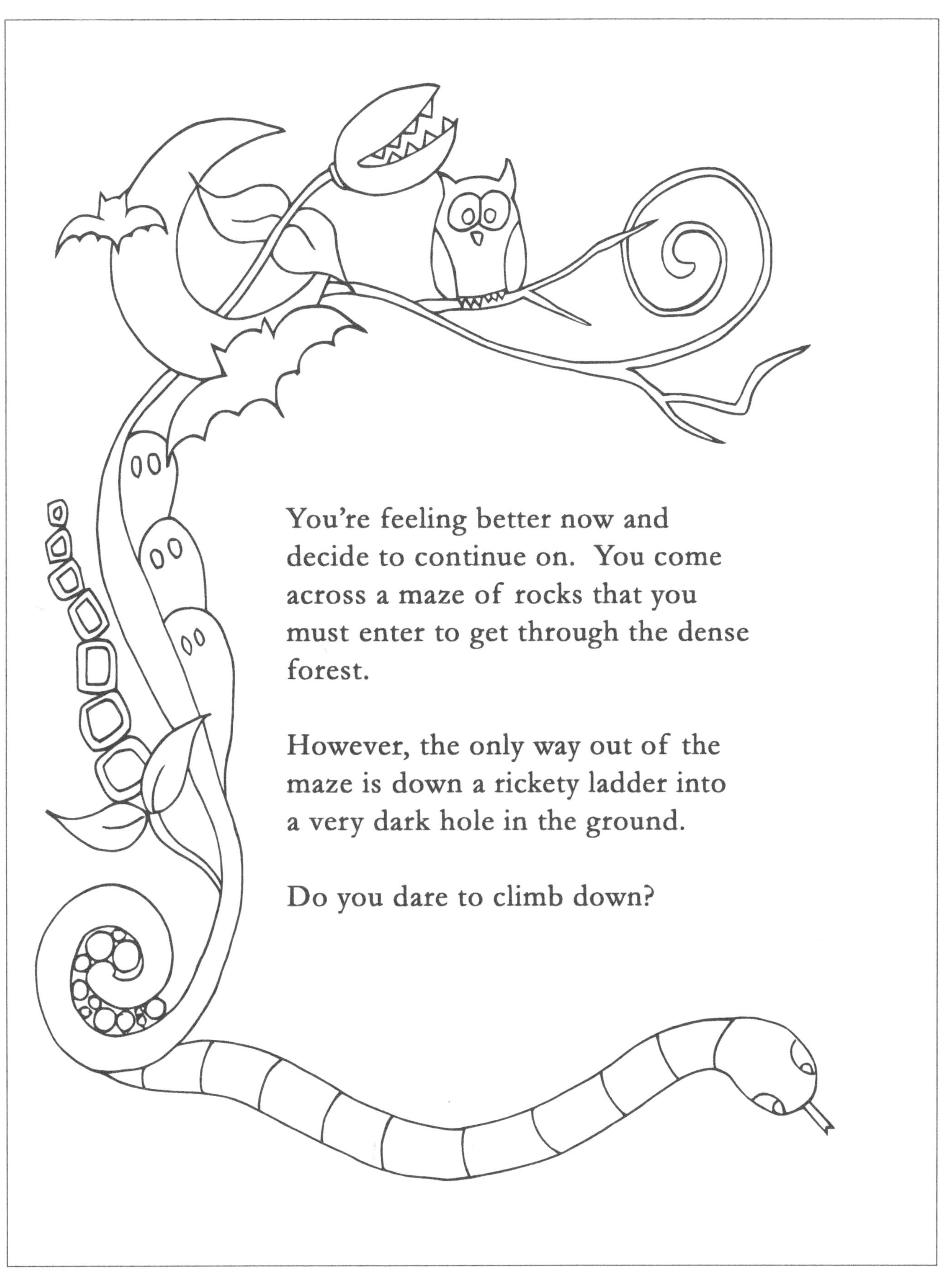

You're feeling better now and decide to continue on. You come across a maze of rocks that you must enter to get through the dense forest.

However, the only way out of the maze is down a rickety ladder into a very dark hole in the ground.

Do you dare to climb down?

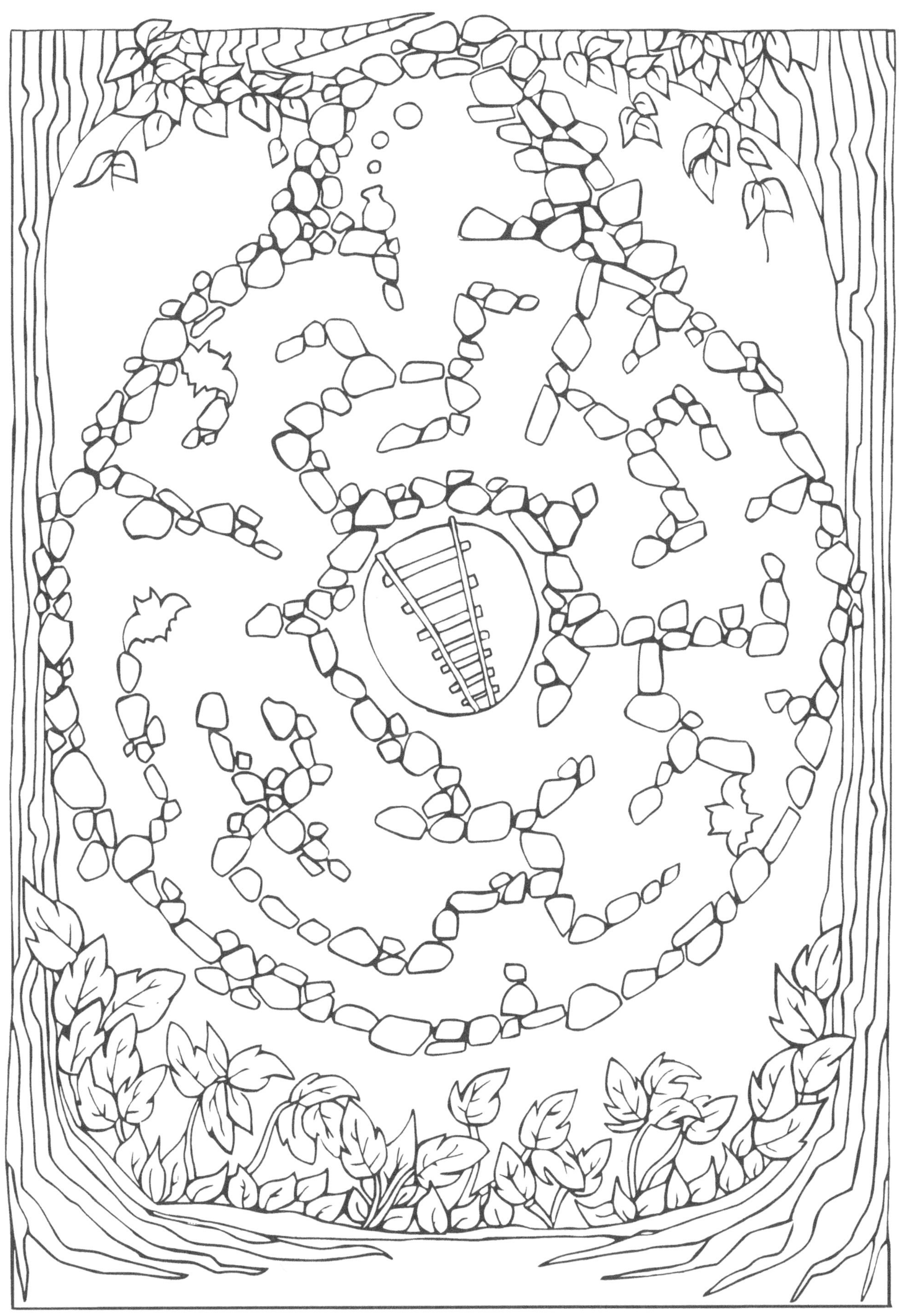

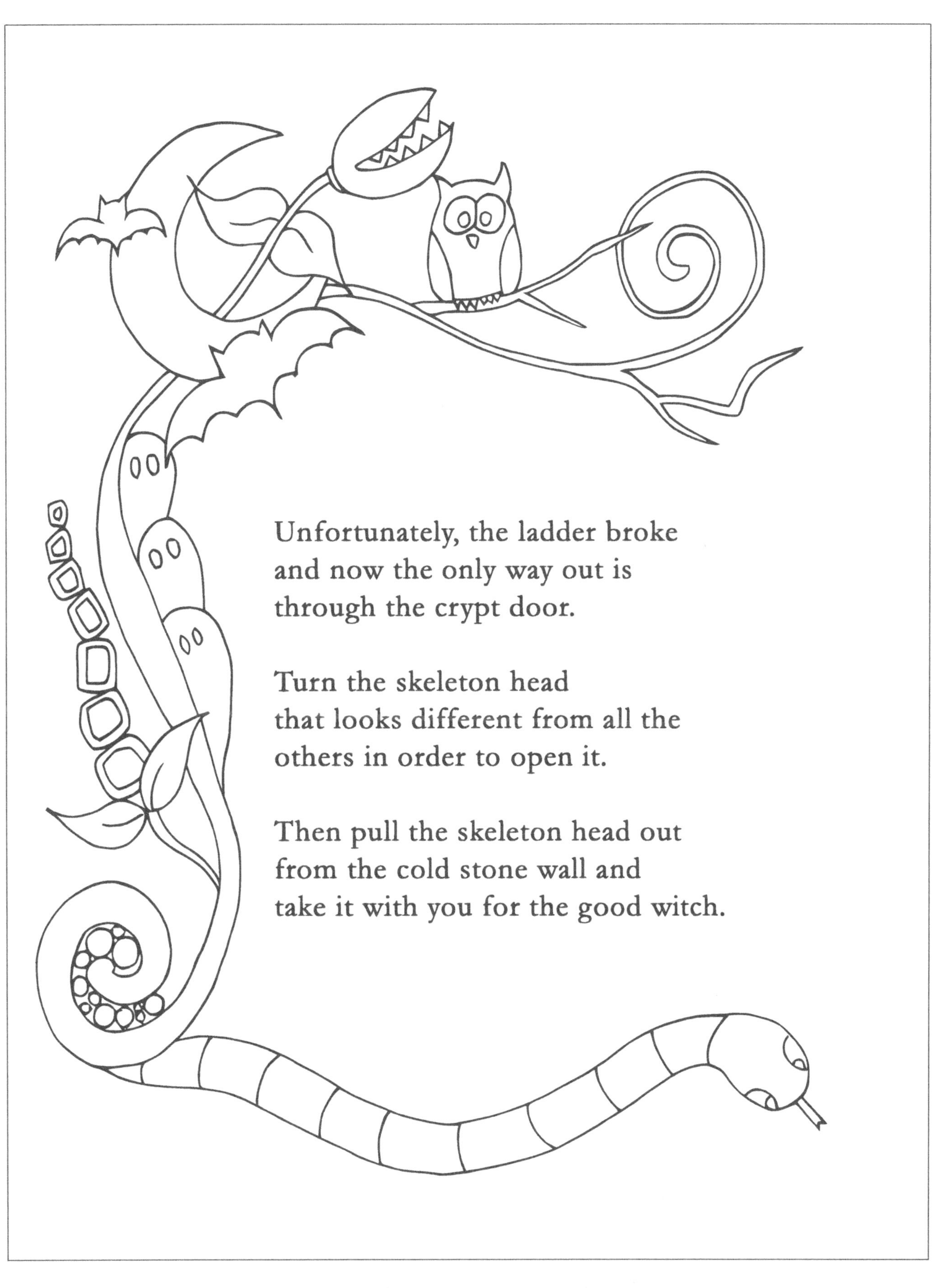

Unfortunately, the ladder broke
and now the only way out is
through the crypt door.

Turn the skeleton head
that looks different from all the
others in order to open it.

Then pull the skeleton head out
from the cold stone wall and
take it with you for the good witch.

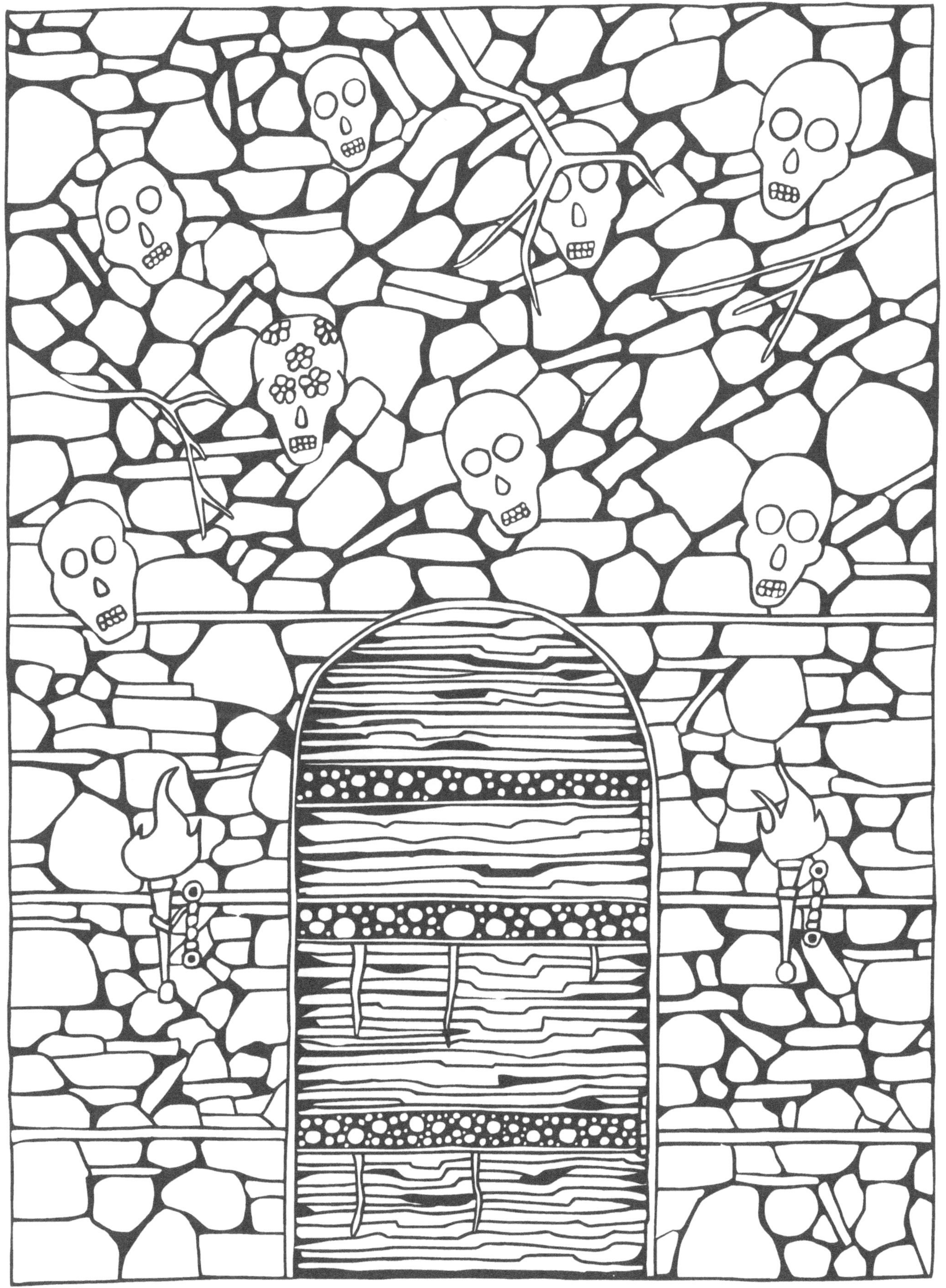

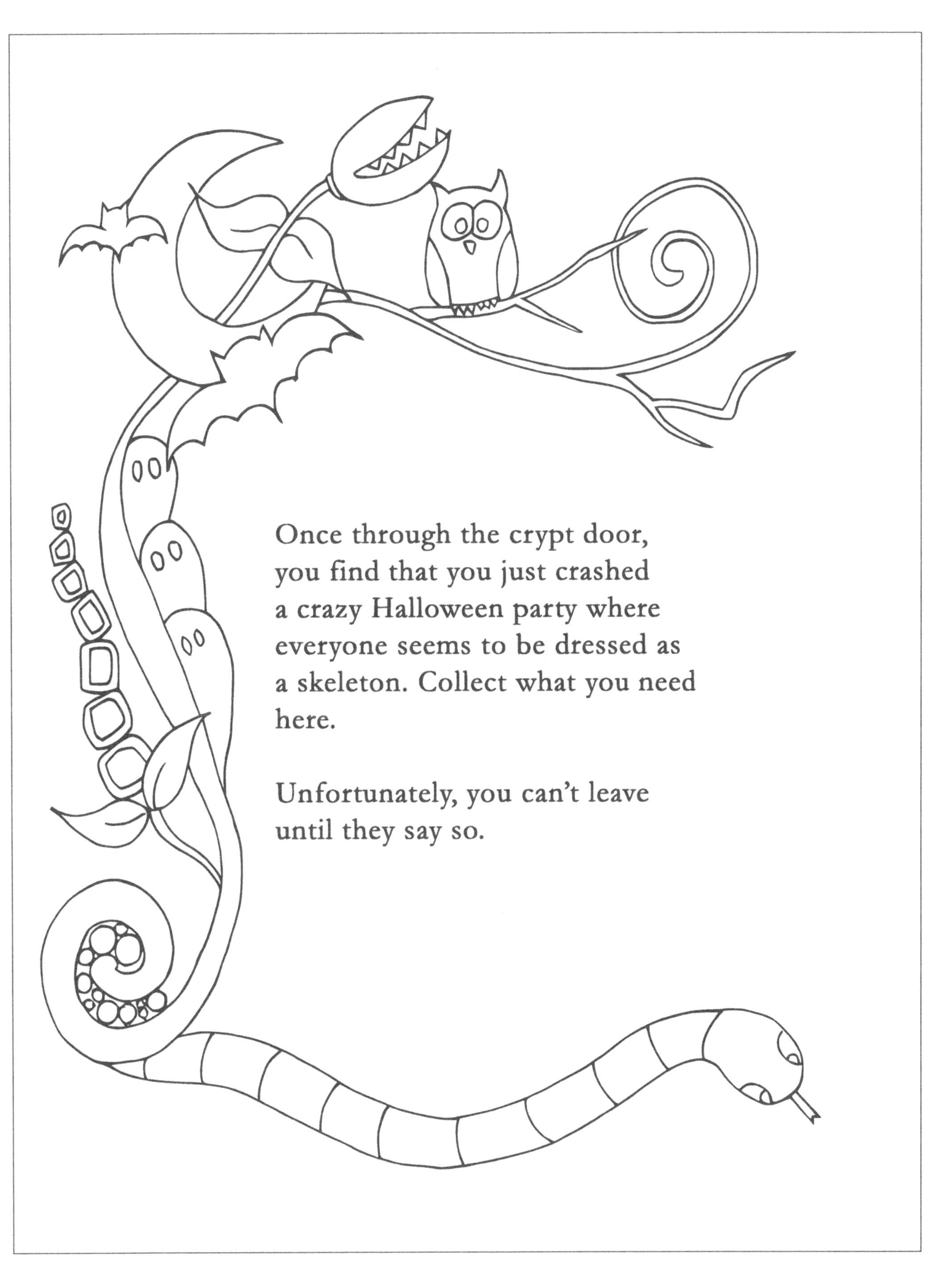

Once through the crypt door, you find that you just crashed a crazy Halloween party where everyone seems to be dressed as a skeleton. Collect what you need here.

Unfortunately, you can't leave until they say so.

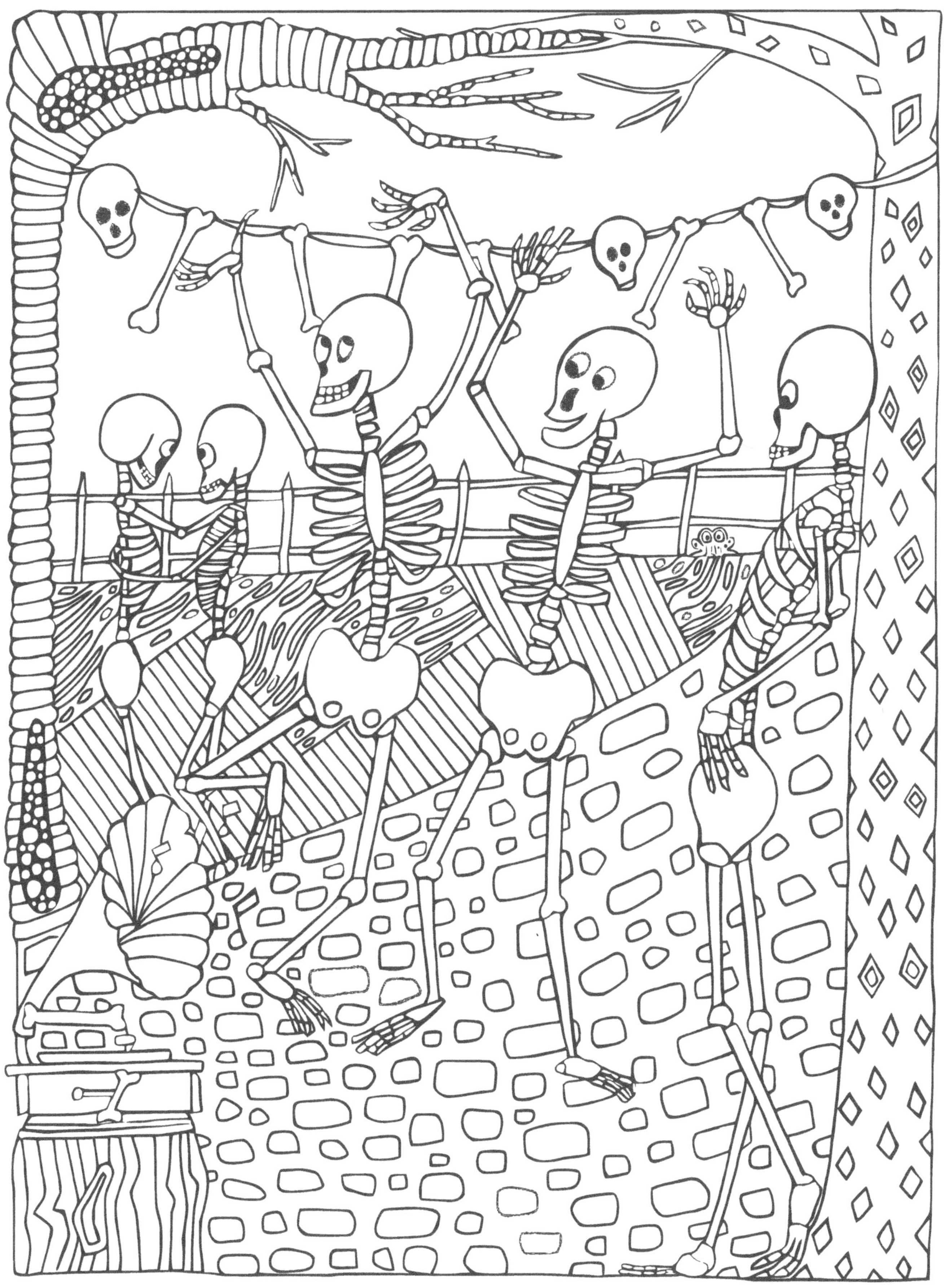

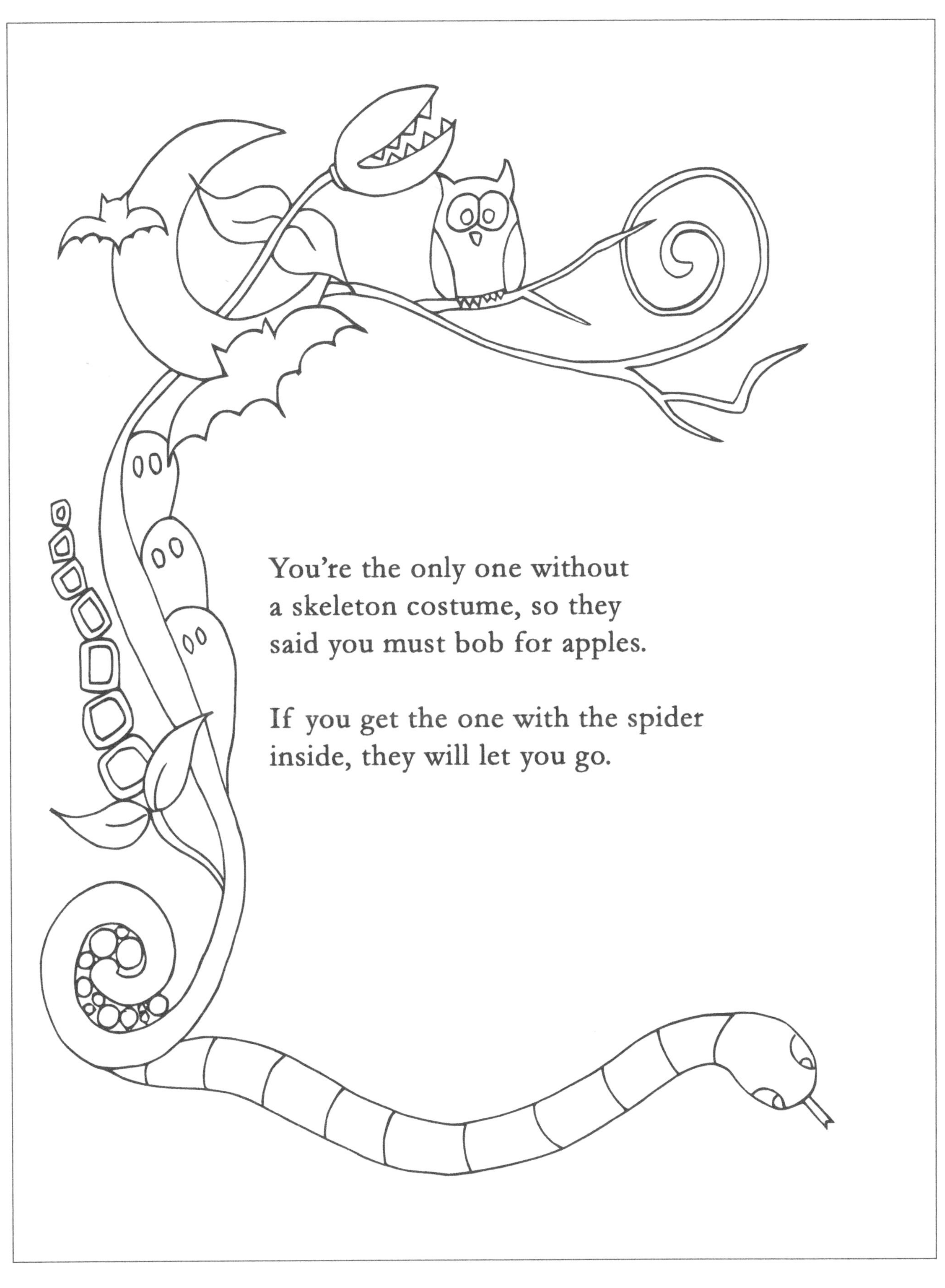

You're the only one without
a skeleton costume, so they
said you must bob for apples.

If you get the one with the spider
inside, they will let you go.

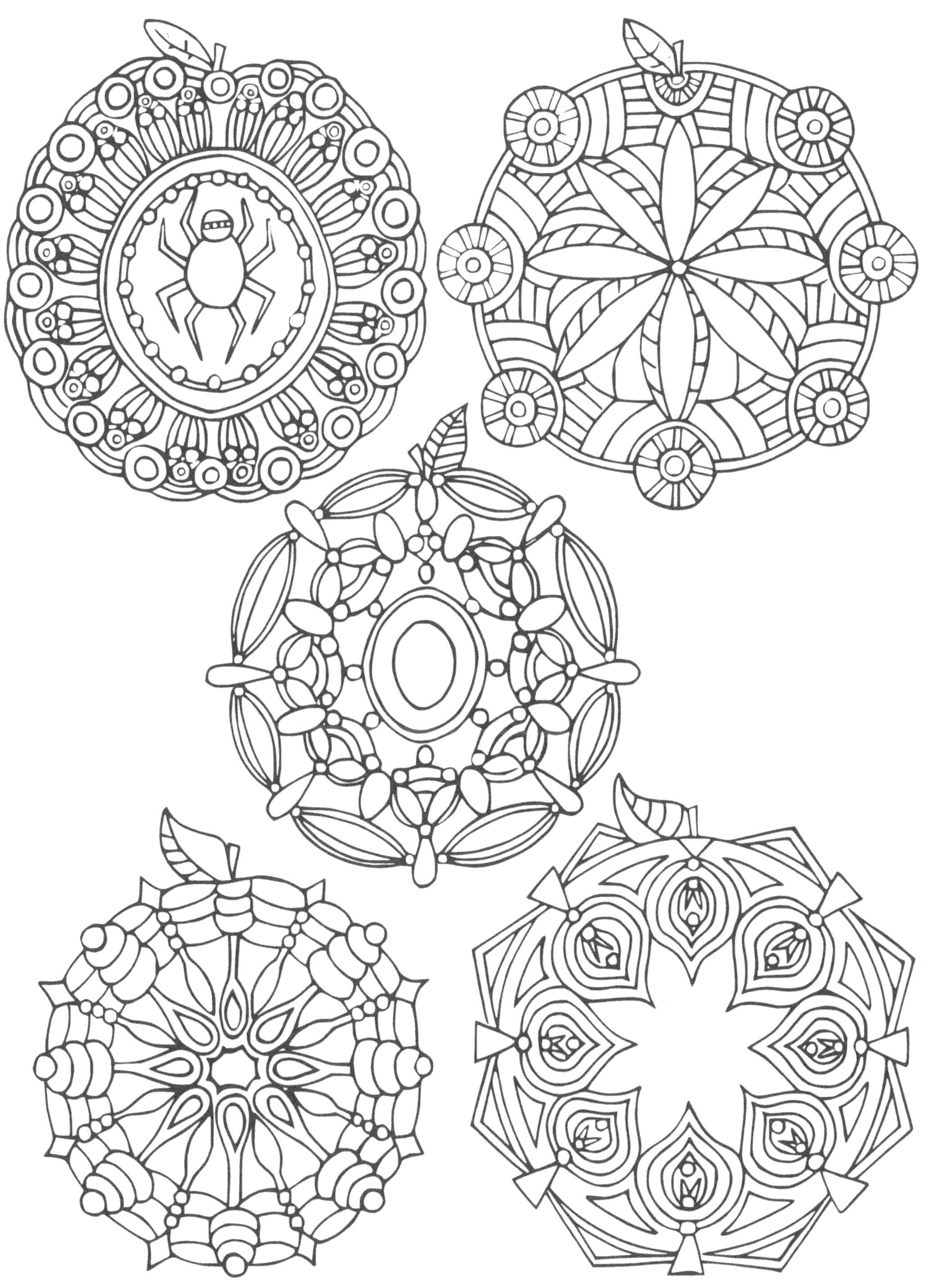

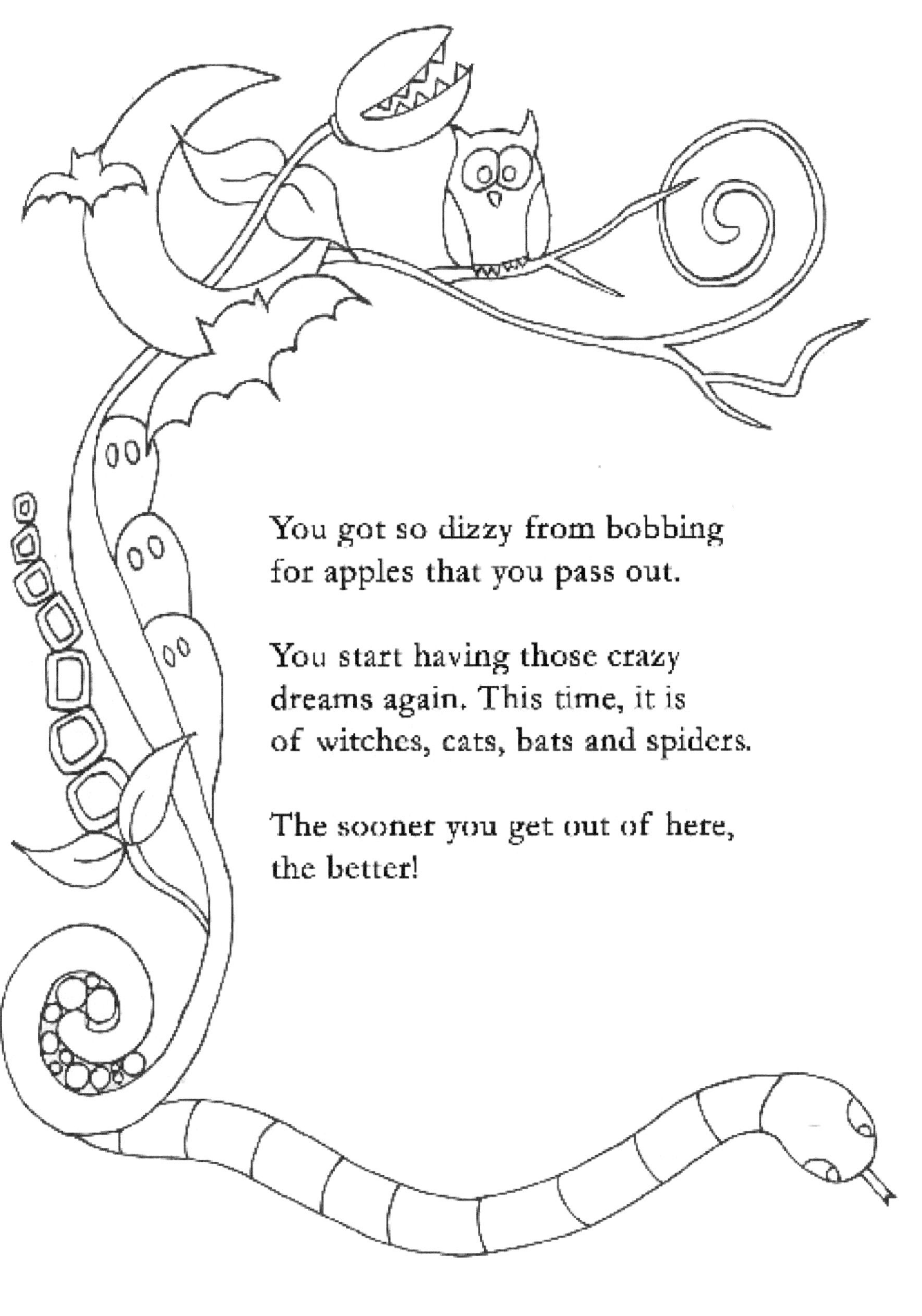

You got so dizzy from bobbing for apples that you pass out.

You start having those crazy dreams again. This time, it is of witches, cats, bats and spiders.

The sooner you get out of here, the better!

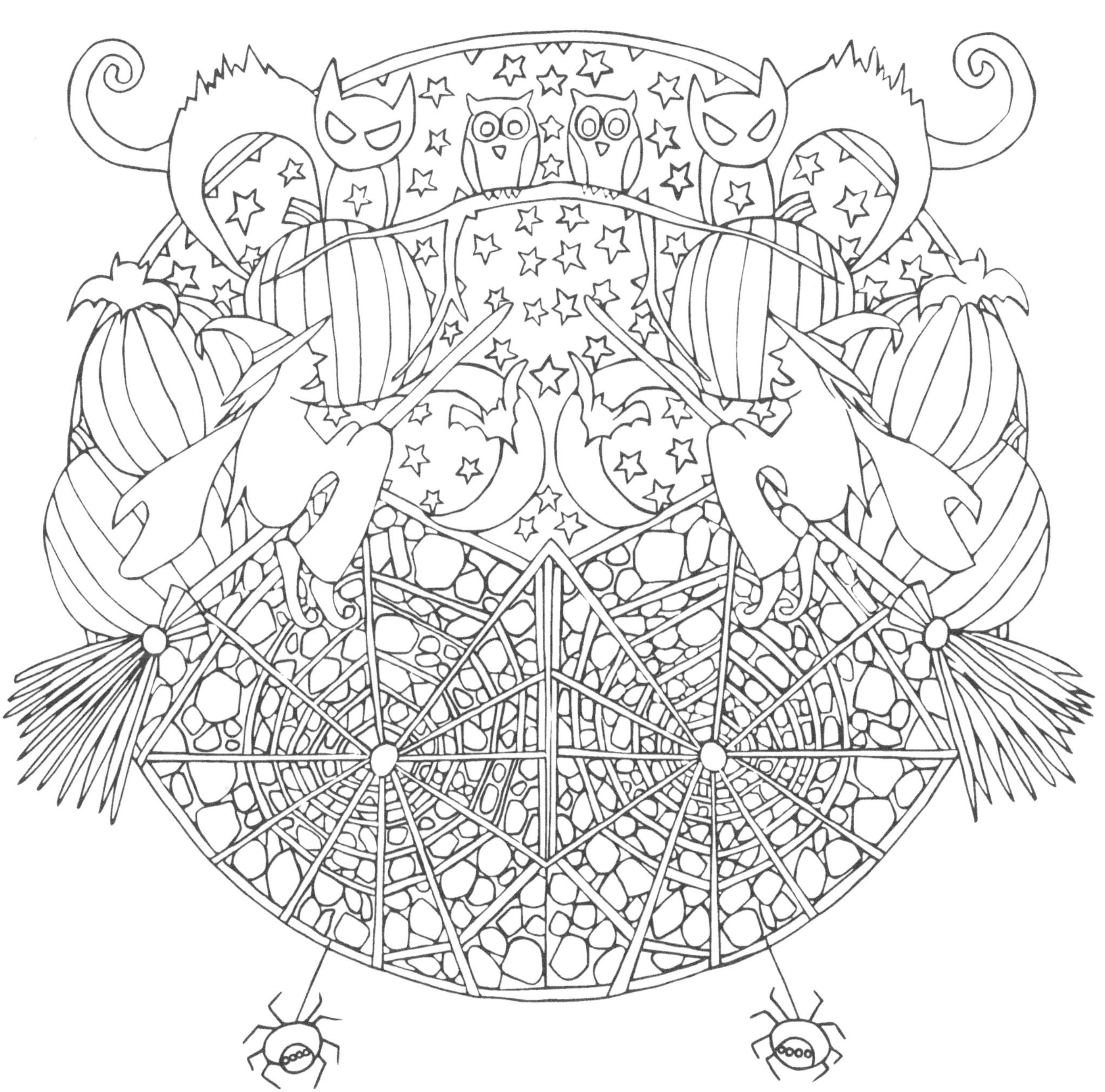

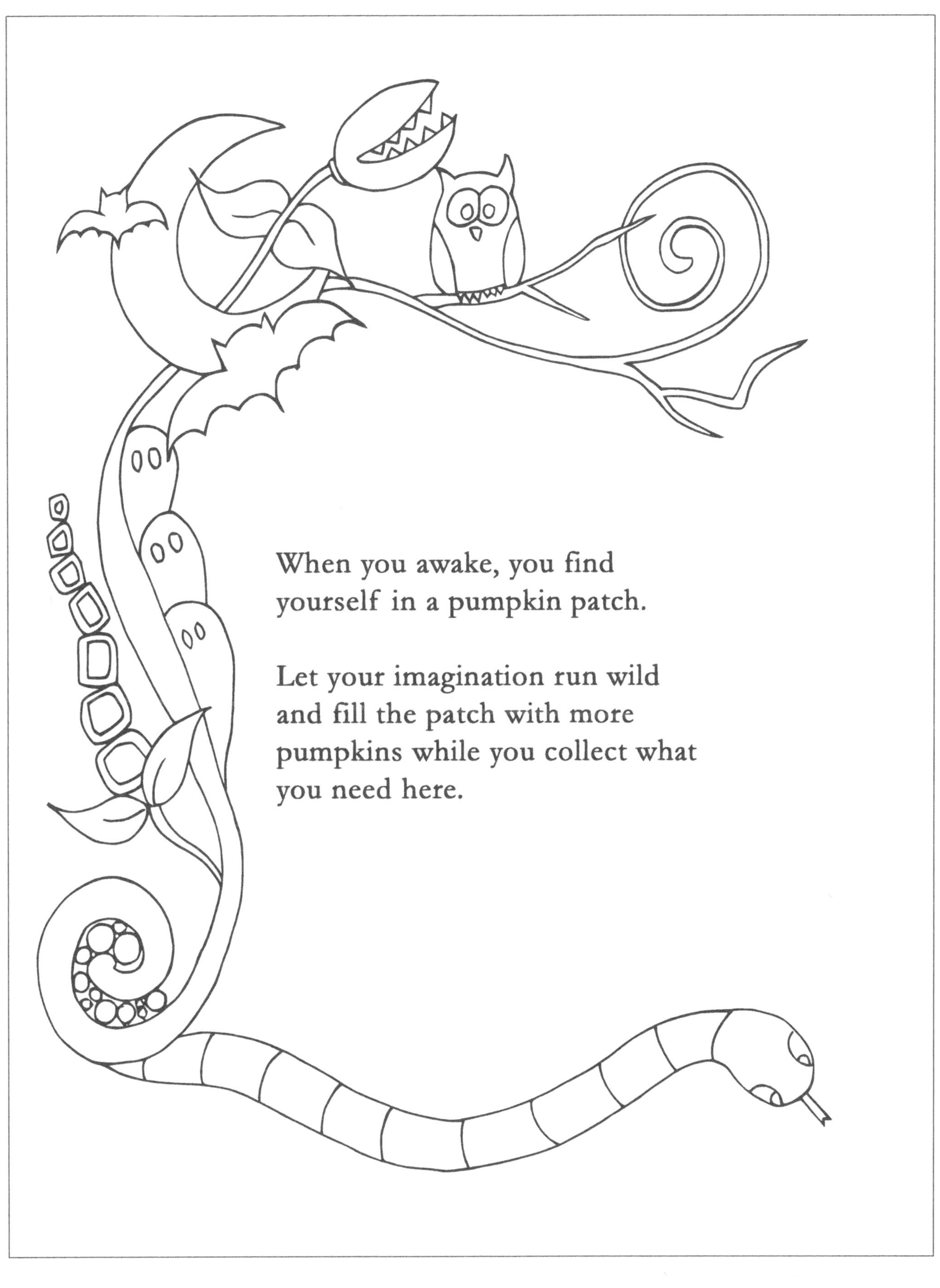

When you awake, you find yourself in a pumpkin patch.

Let your imagination run wild and fill the patch with more pumpkins while you collect what you need here.

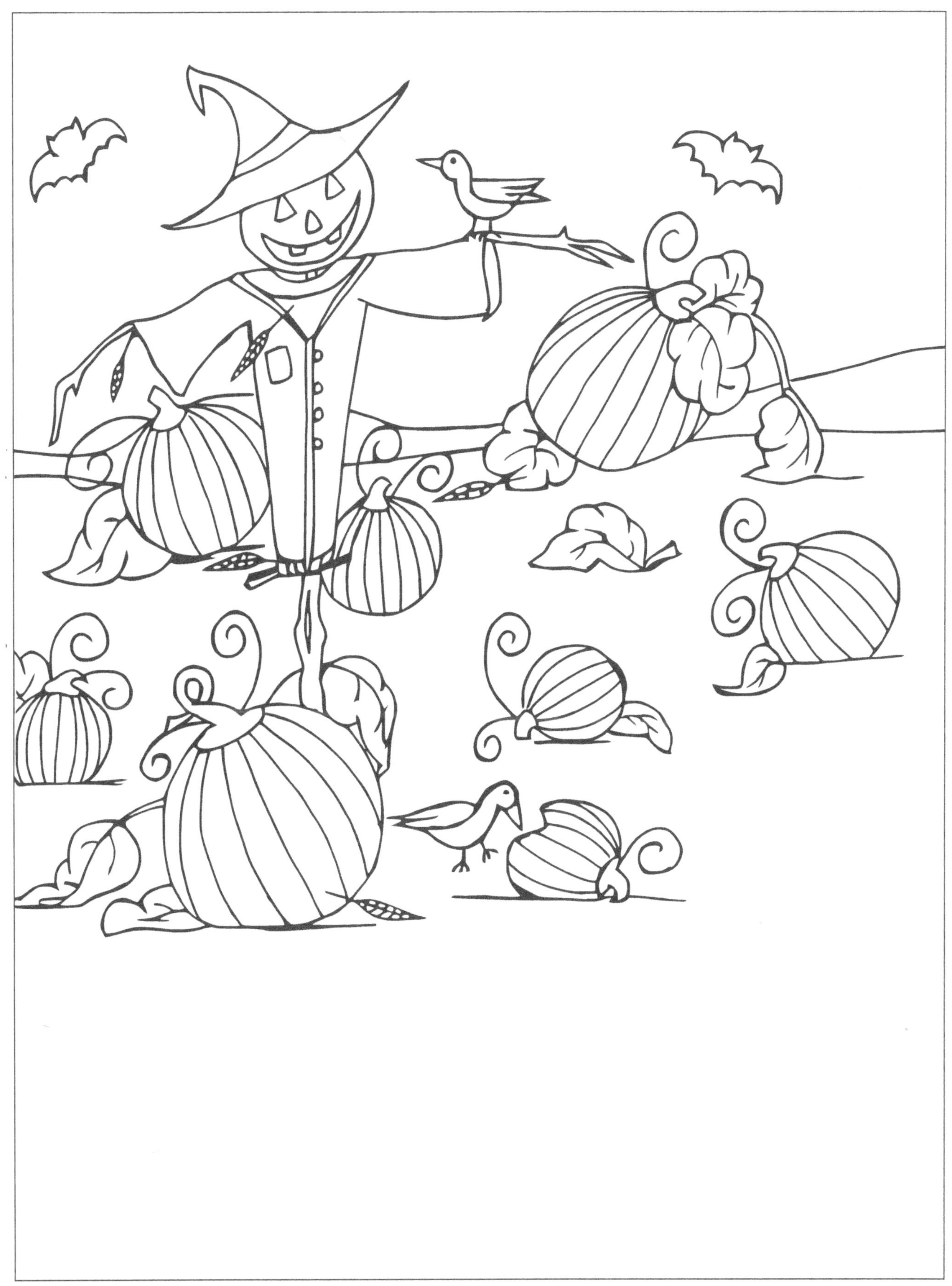

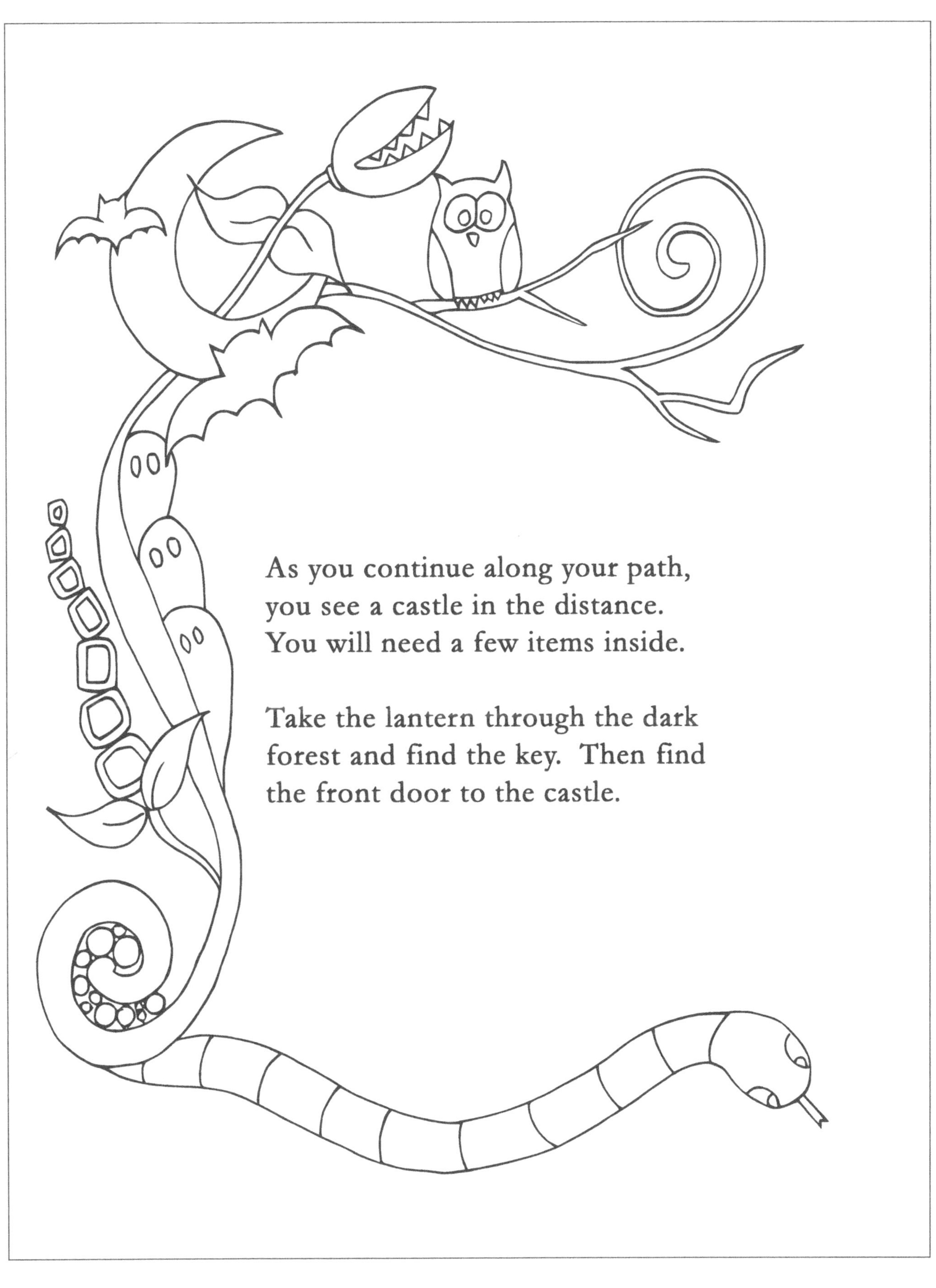

As you continue along your path, you see a castle in the distance. You will need a few items inside.

Take the lantern through the dark forest and find the key. Then find the front door to the castle.

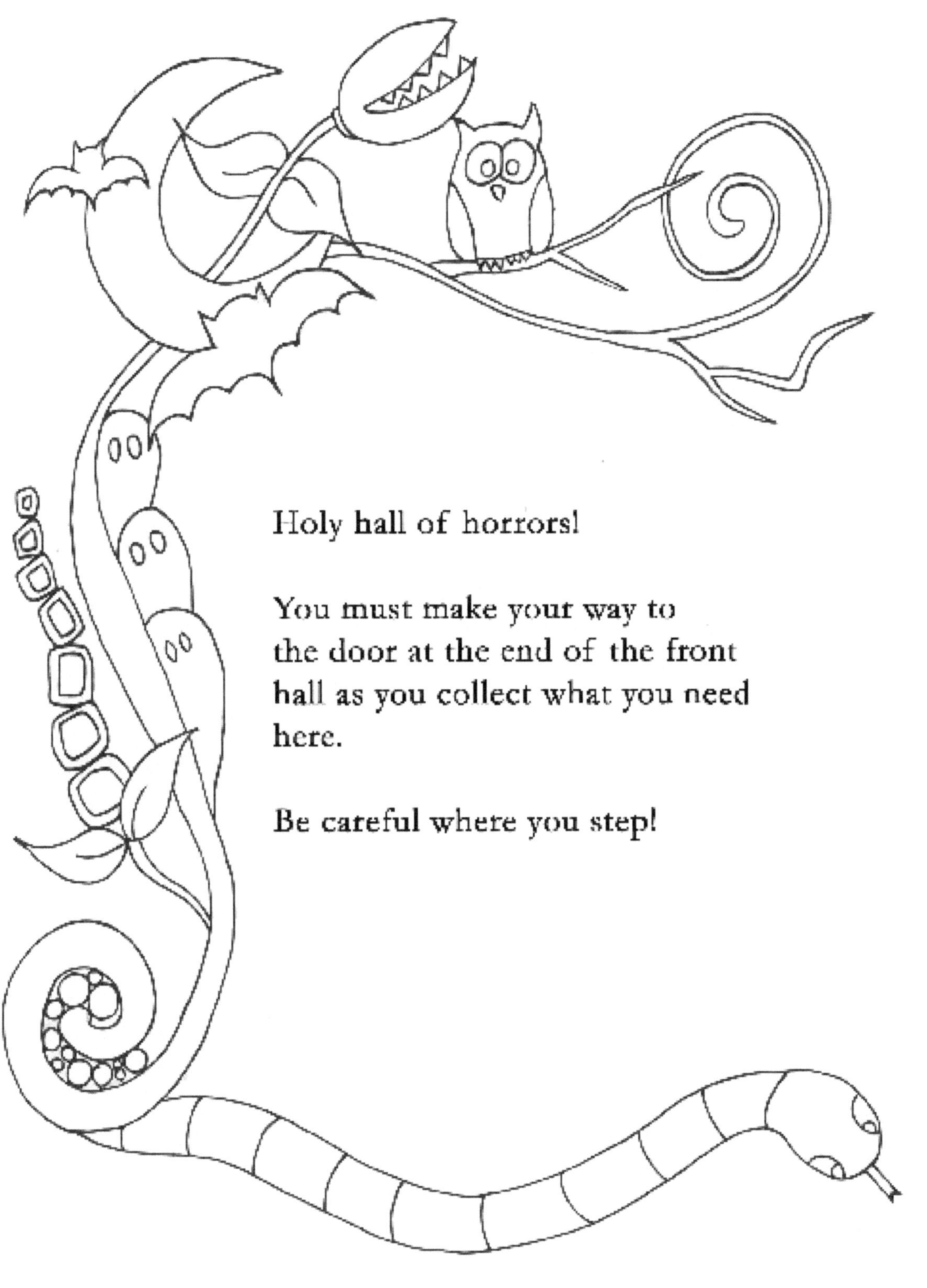

Holy hall of horrors!

You must make your way to the door at the end of the front hall as you collect what you need here.

Be careful where you step!

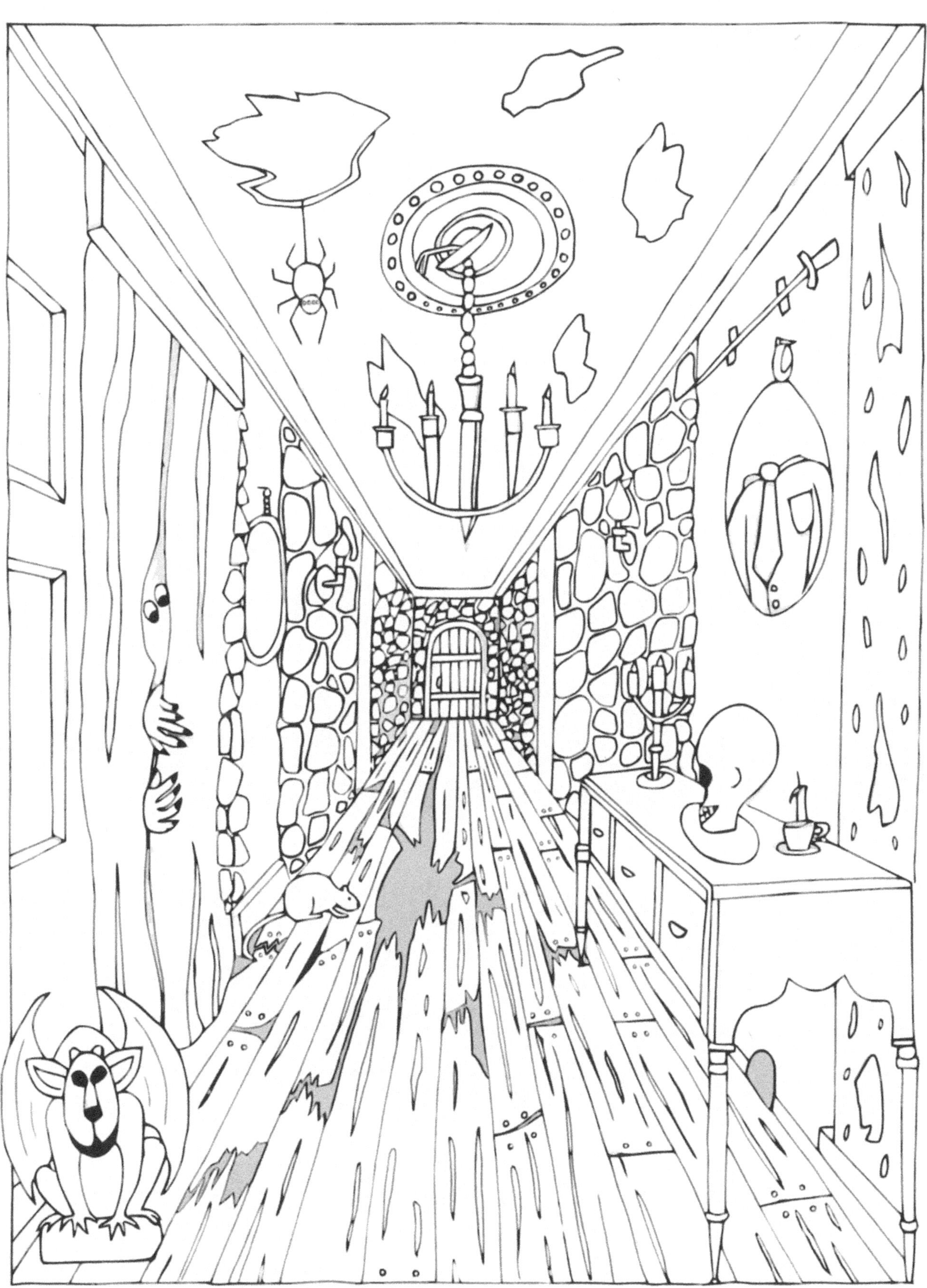

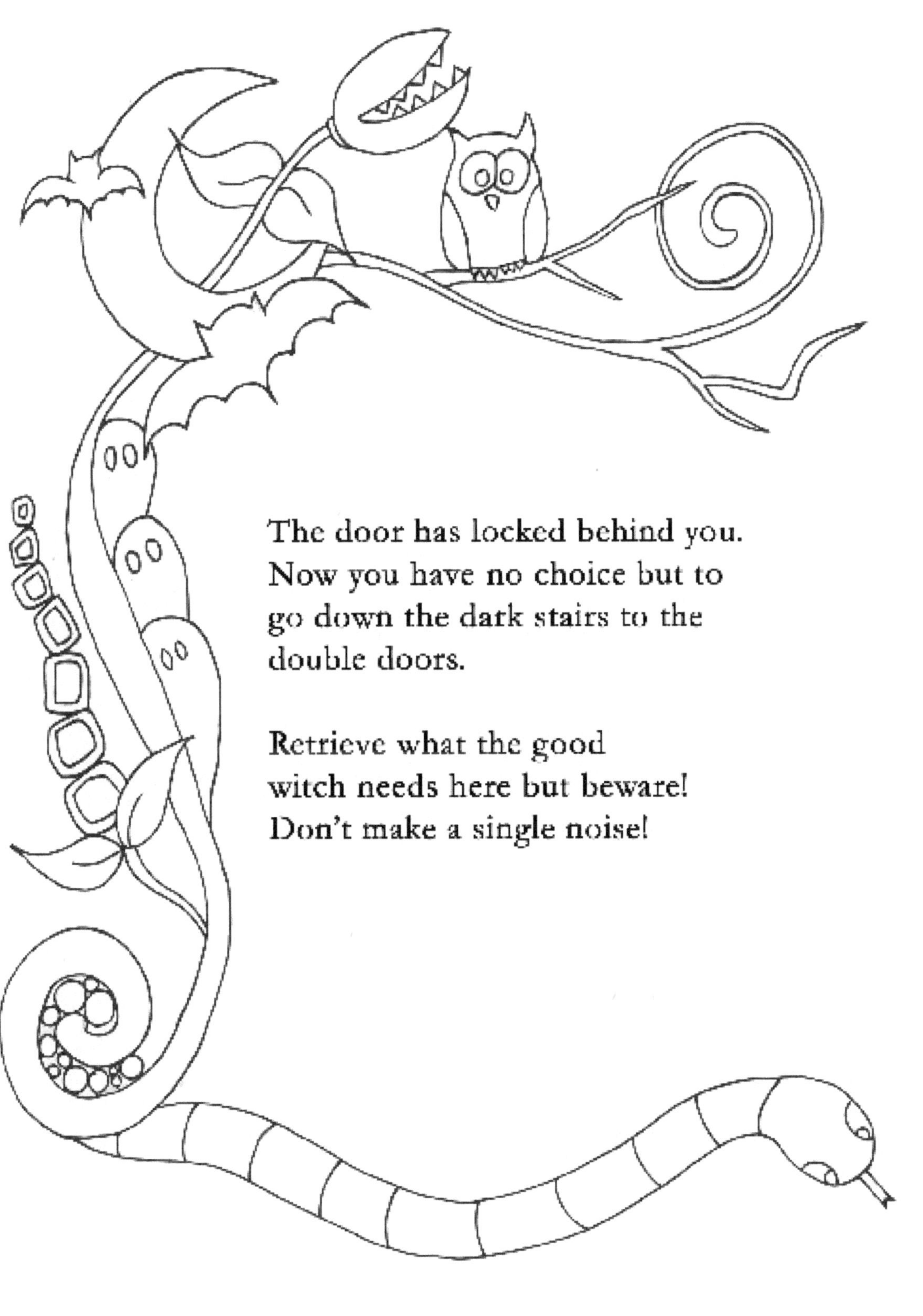

The door has locked behind you. Now you have no choice but to go down the dark stairs to the double doors.

Retrieve what the good witch needs here but beware! Don't make a single noise!

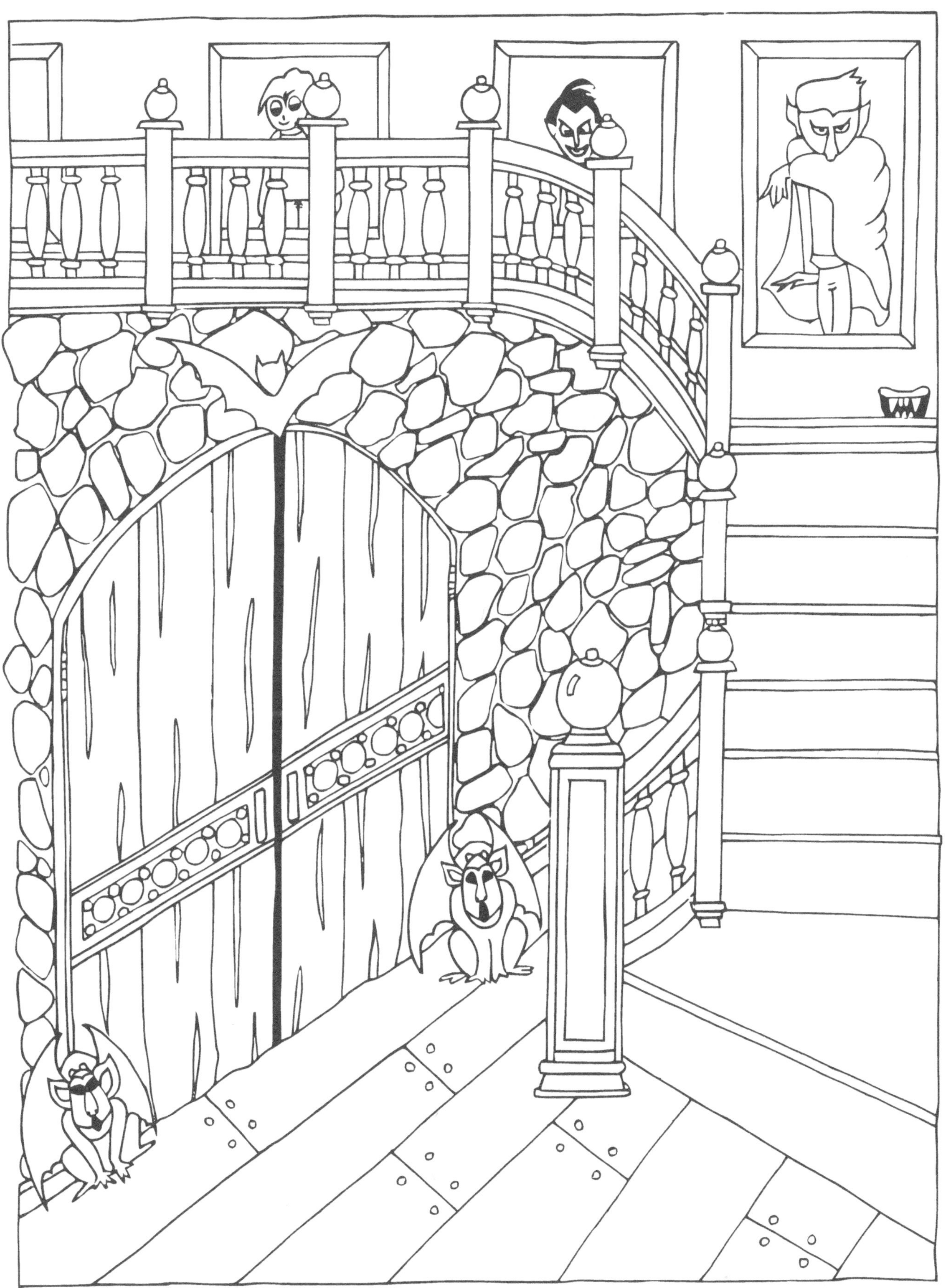

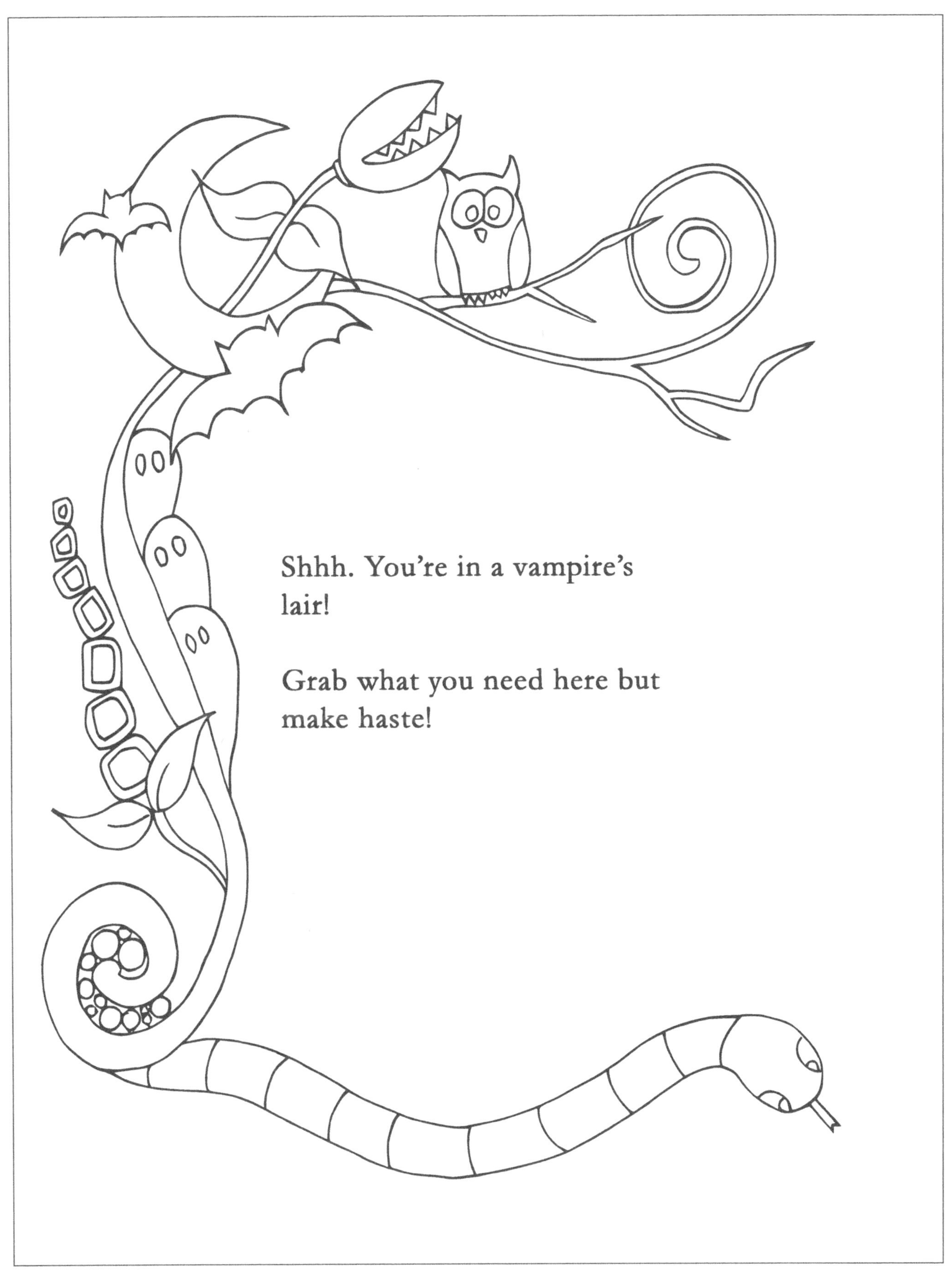

Shhh. You're in a vampire's lair!

Grab what you need here but make haste!

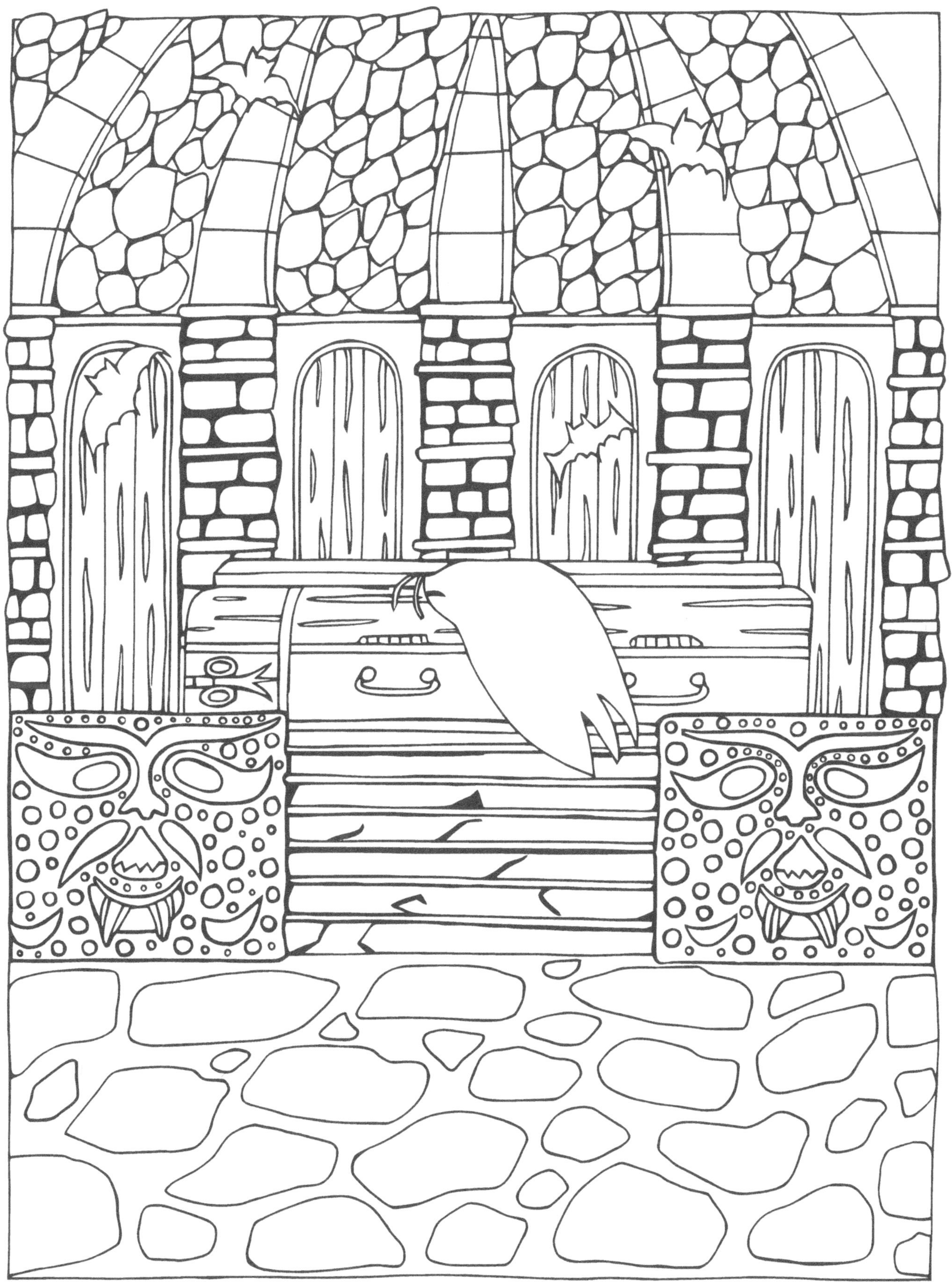

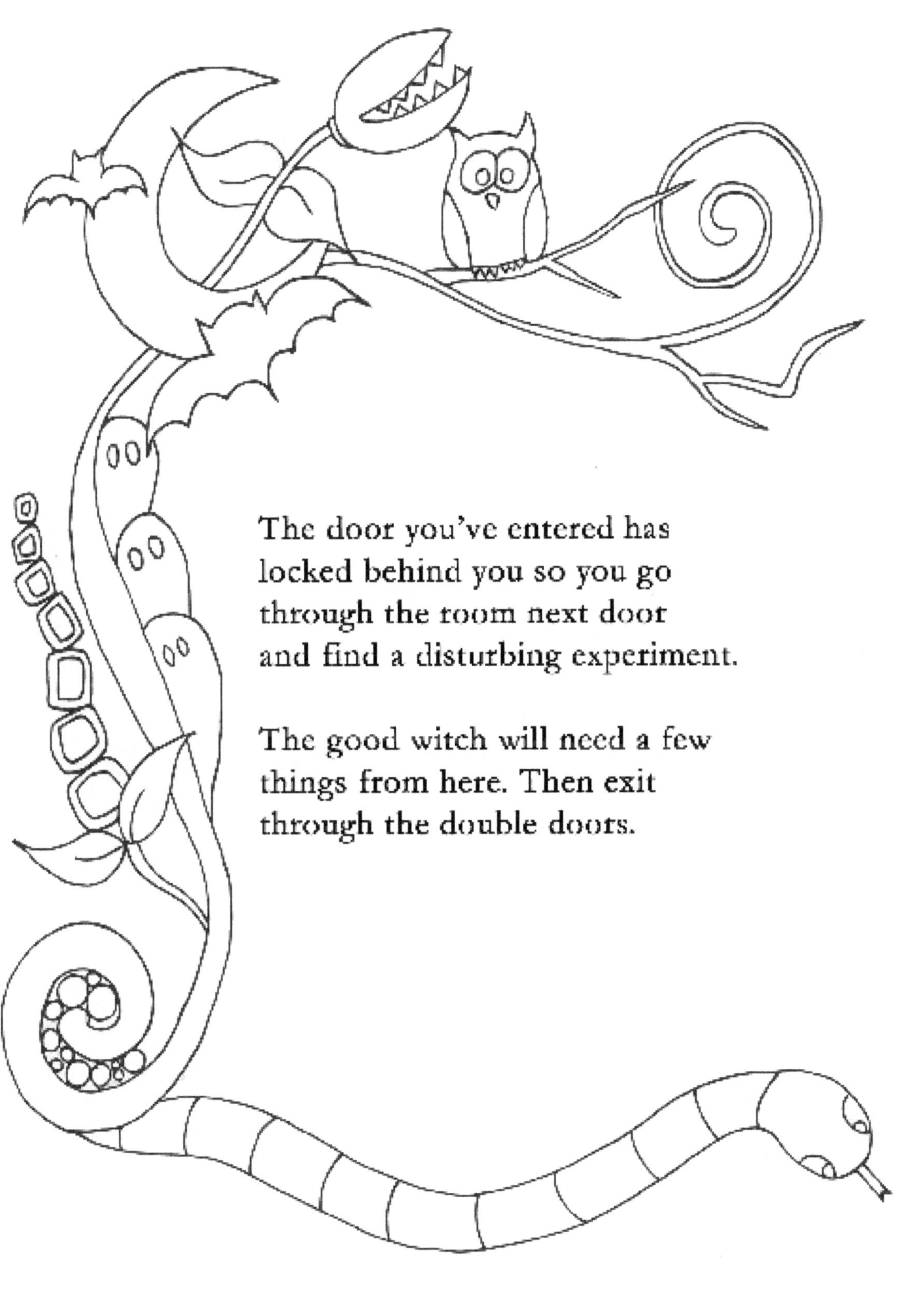

The door you've entered has
locked behind you so you go
through the room next door
and find a disturbing experiment.

The good witch will need a few
things from here. Then exit
through the double doors.

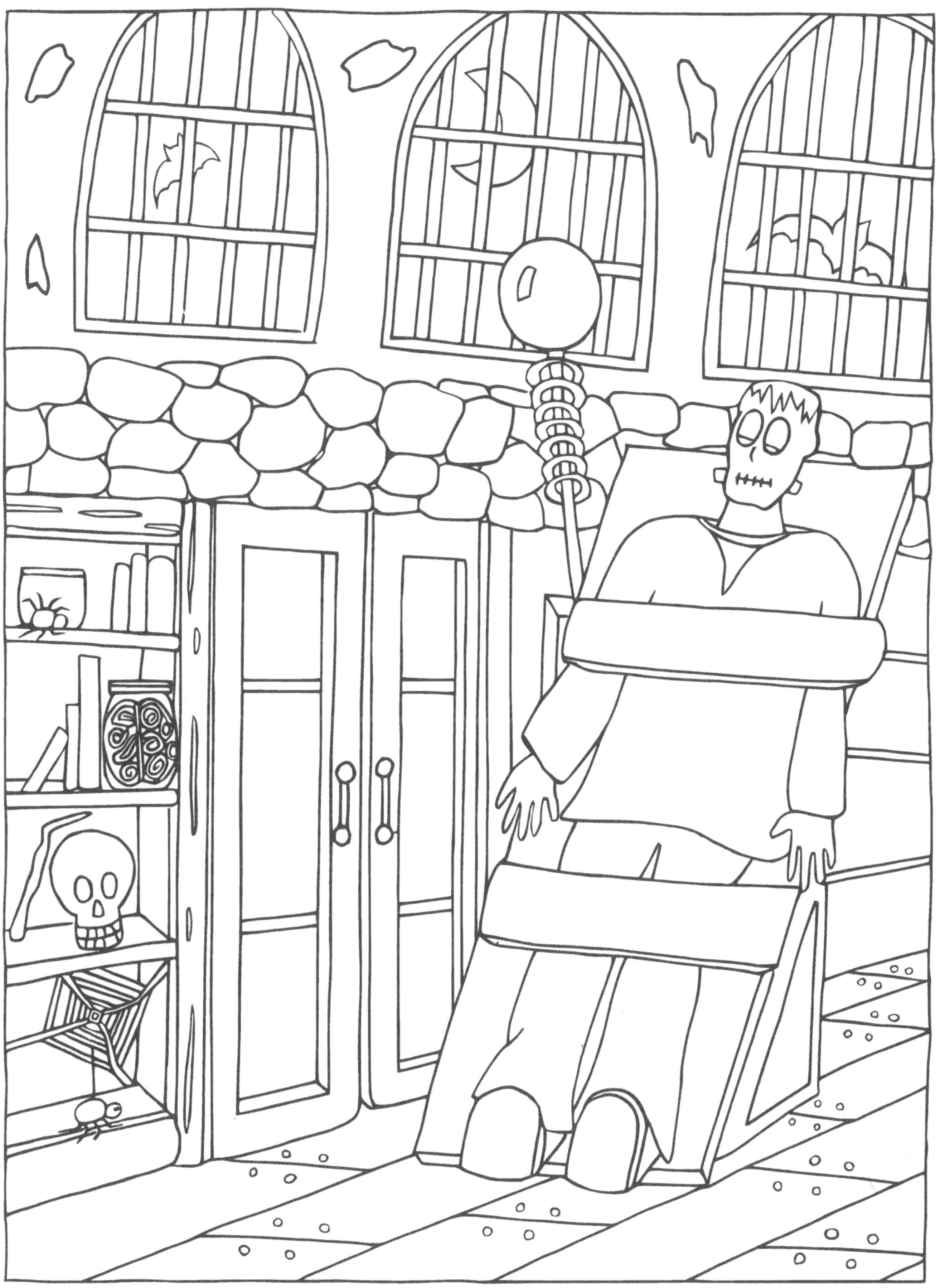

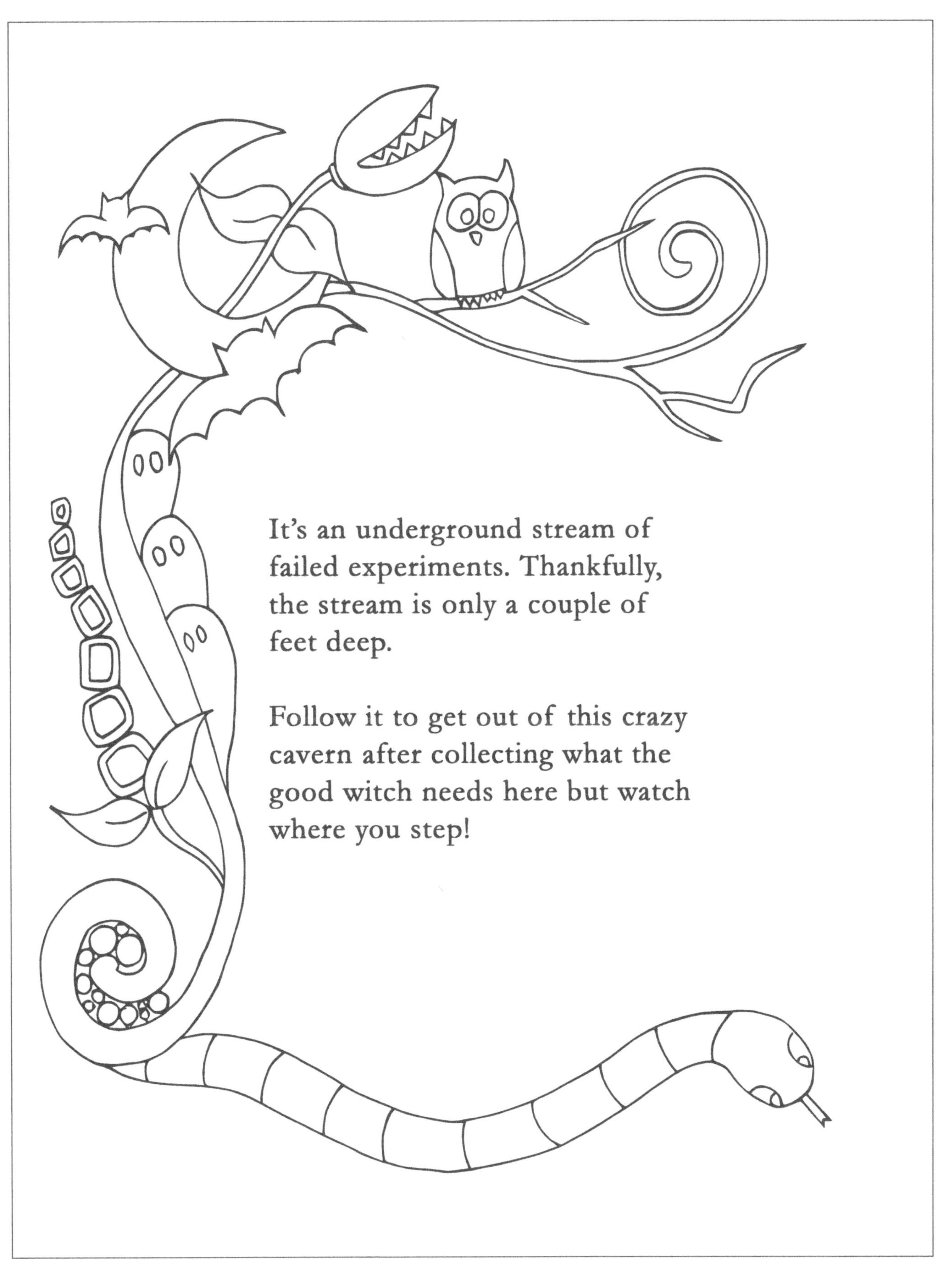

It's an underground stream of failed experiments. Thankfully, the stream is only a couple of feet deep.

Follow it to get out of this crazy cavern after collecting what the good witch needs here but watch where you step!

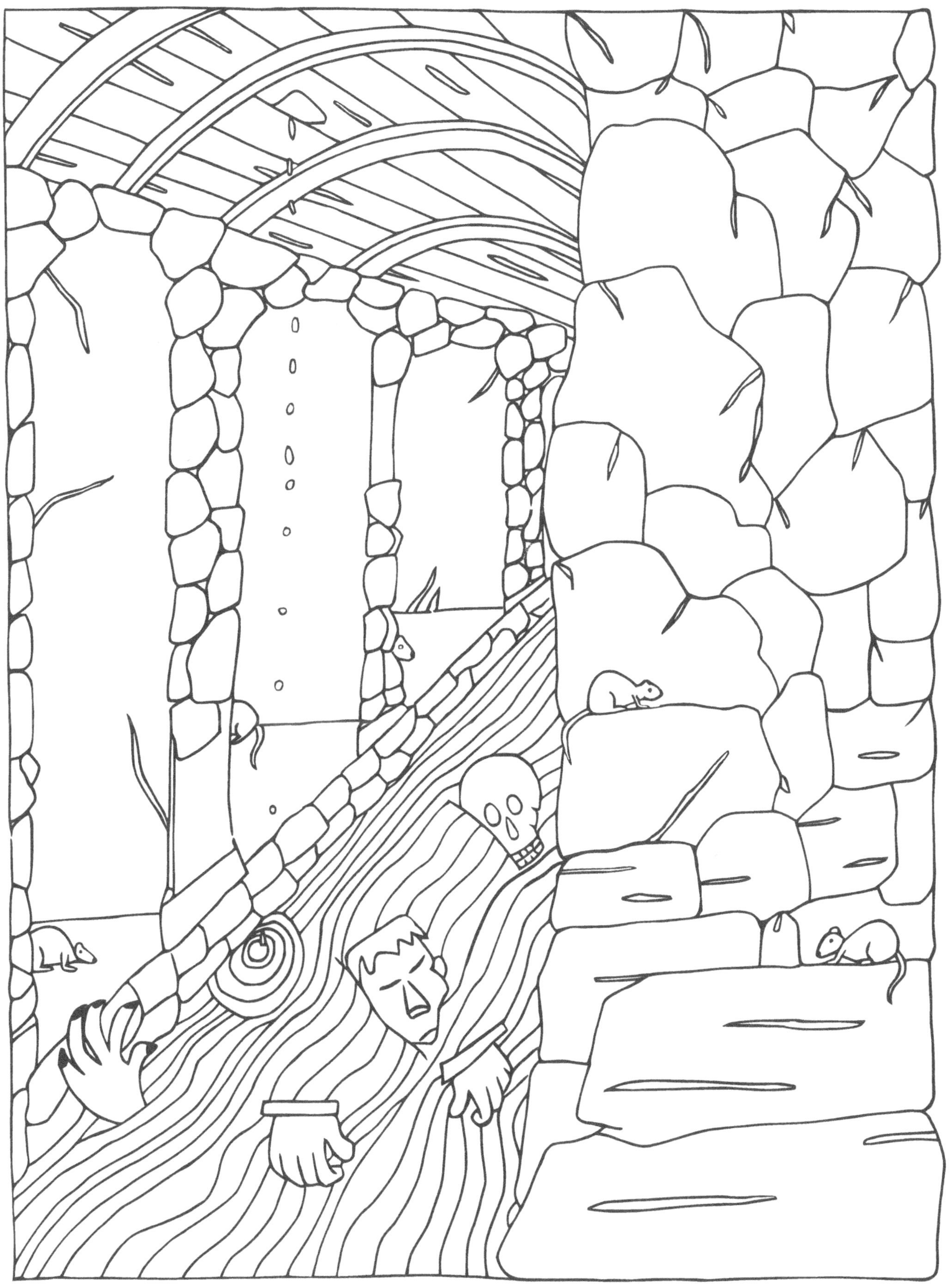

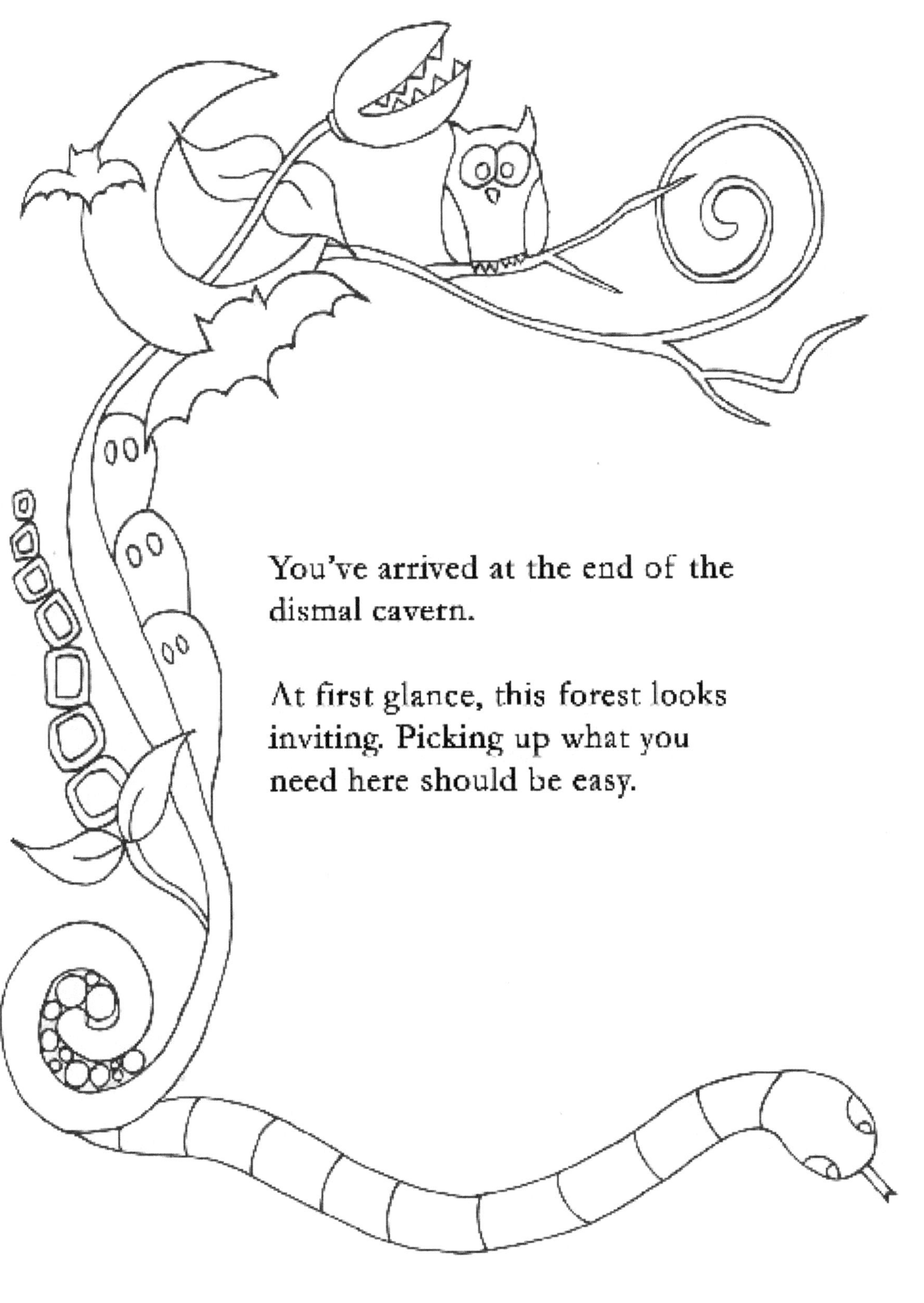

You've arrived at the end of the dismal cavern.

At first glance, this forest looks inviting. Picking up what you need here should be easy.

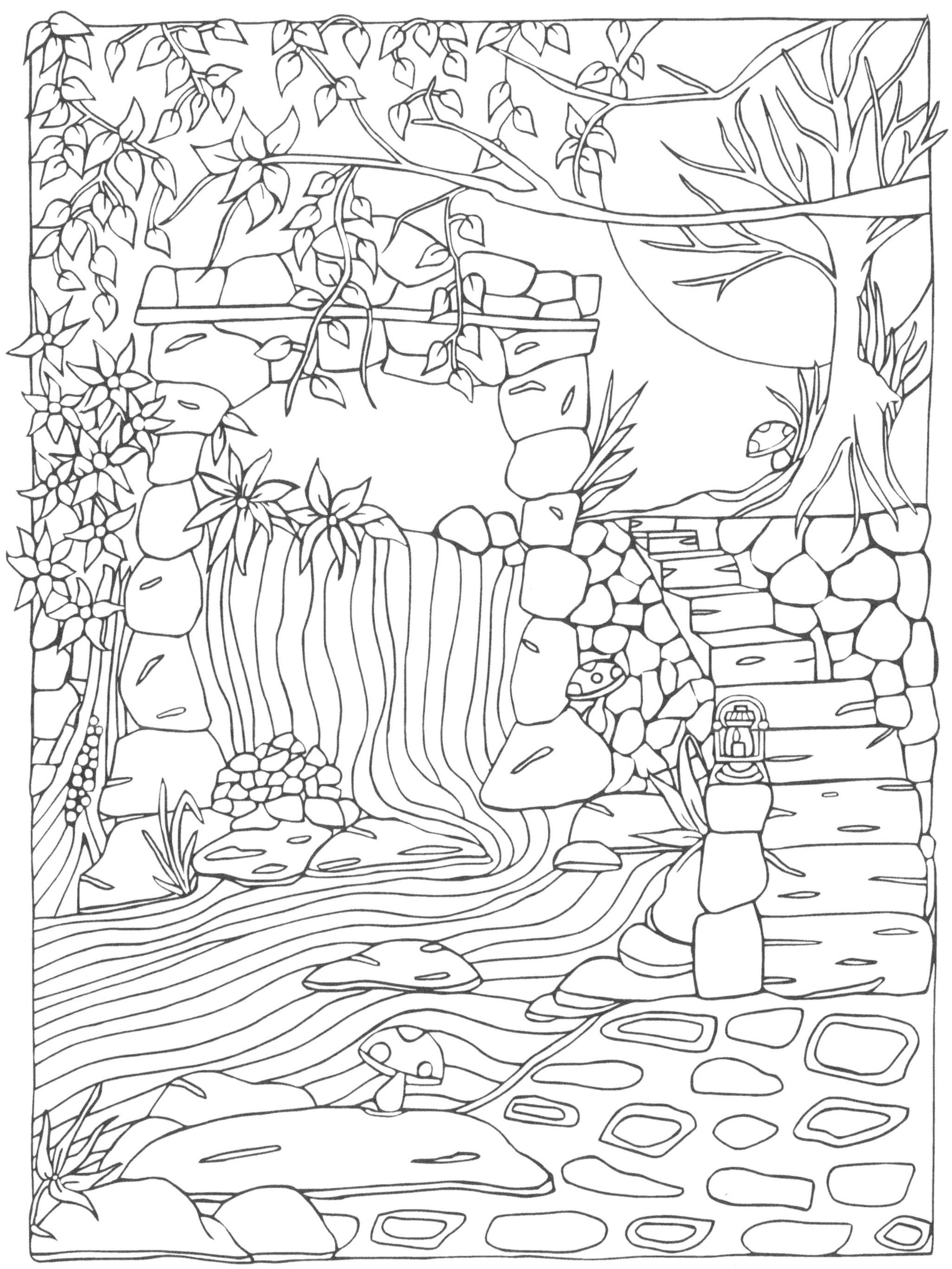

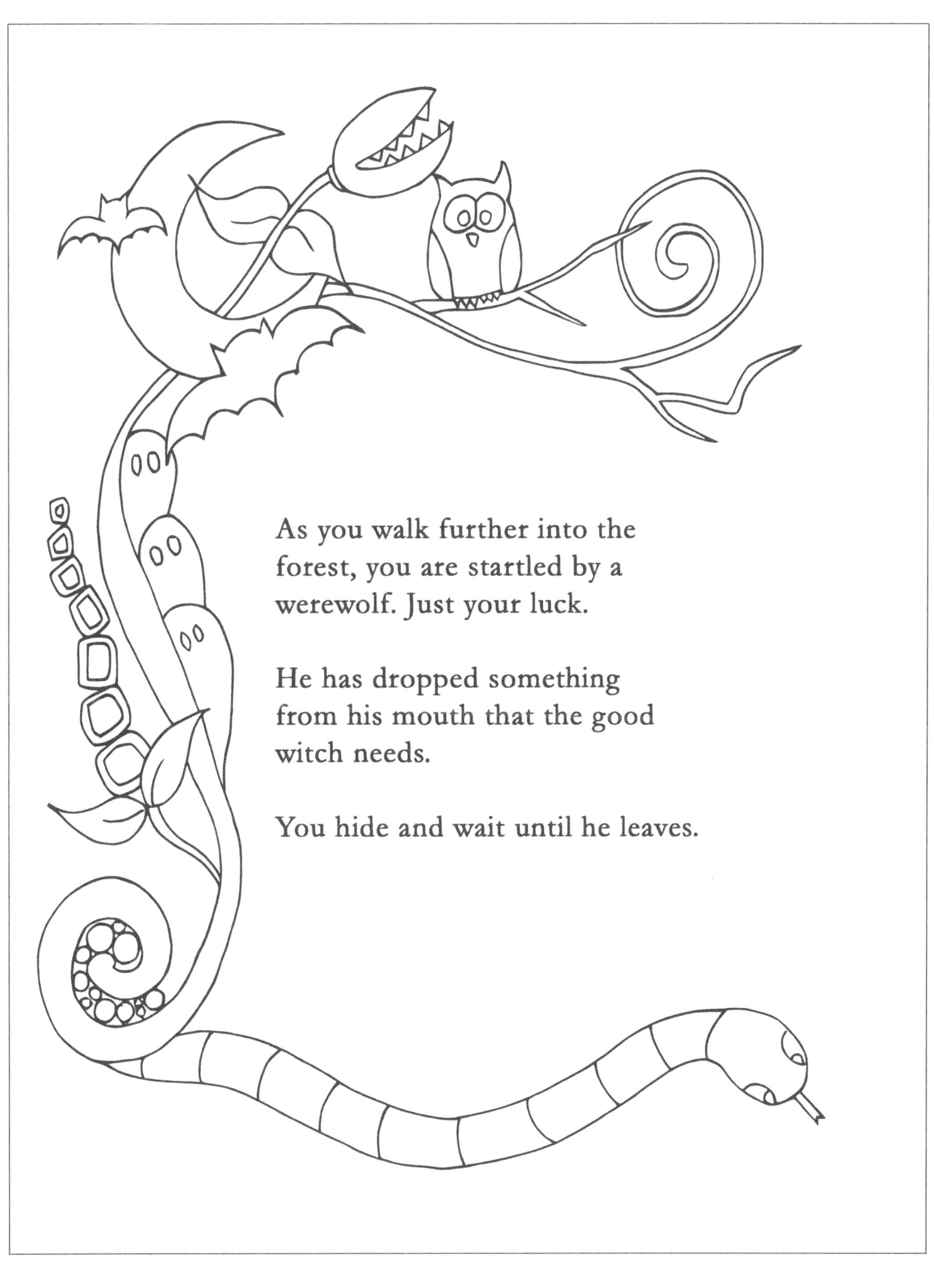

As you walk further into the forest, you are startled by a werewolf. Just your luck.

He has dropped something from his mouth that the good witch needs.

You hide and wait until he leaves.

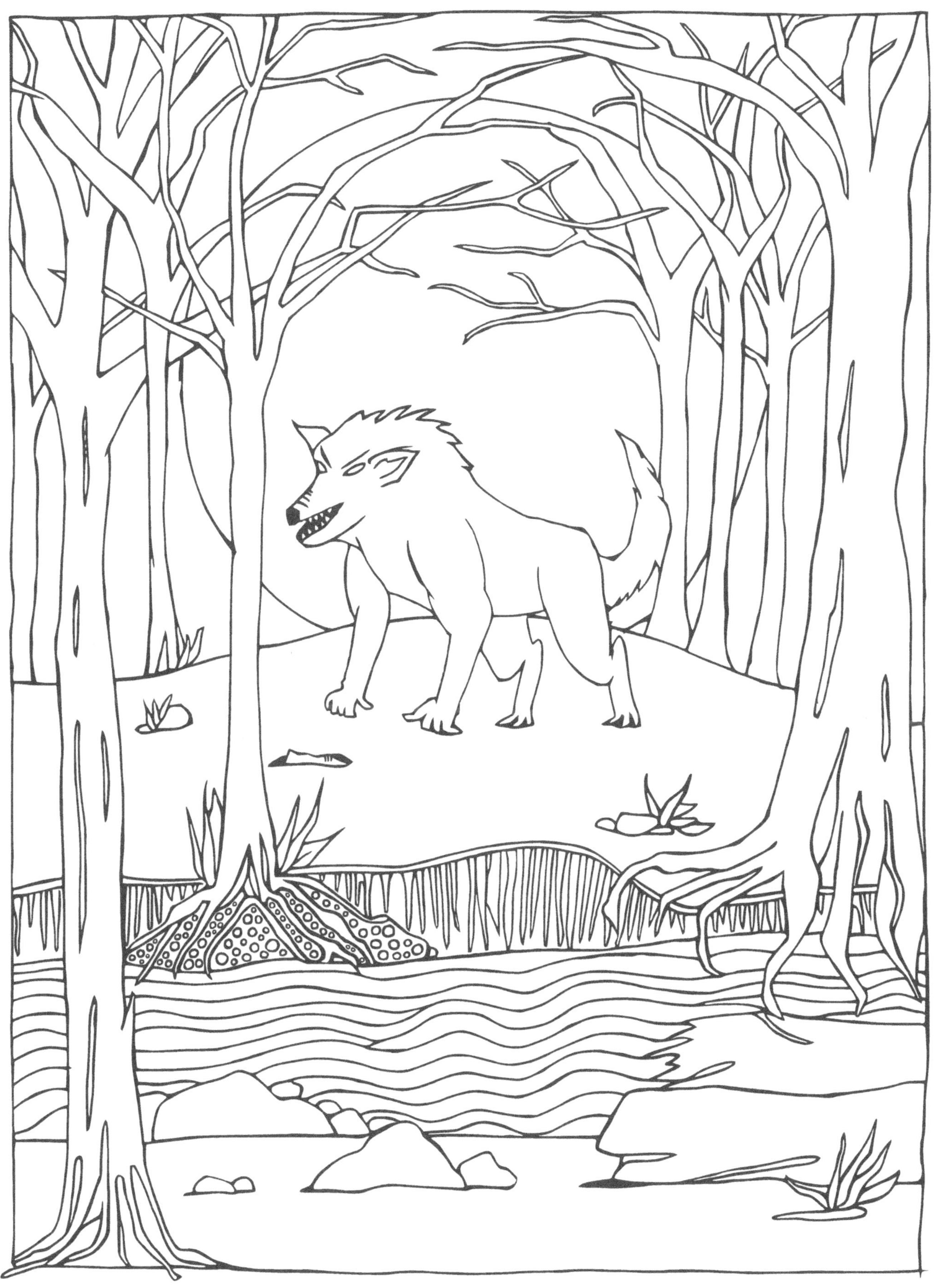

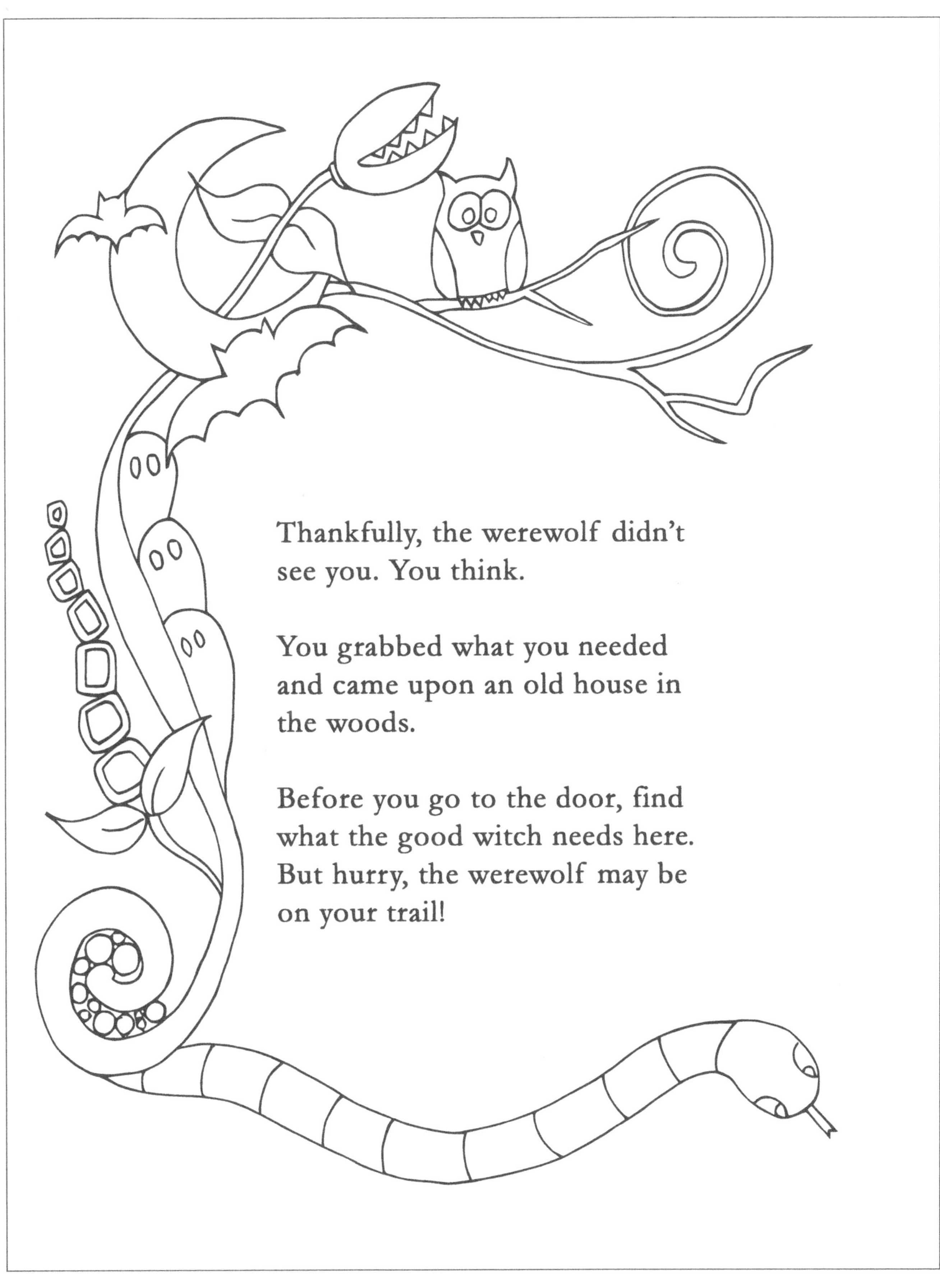

Thankfully, the werewolf didn't see you. You think.

You grabbed what you needed and came upon an old house in the woods.

Before you go to the door, find what the good witch needs here. But hurry, the werewolf may be on your trail!

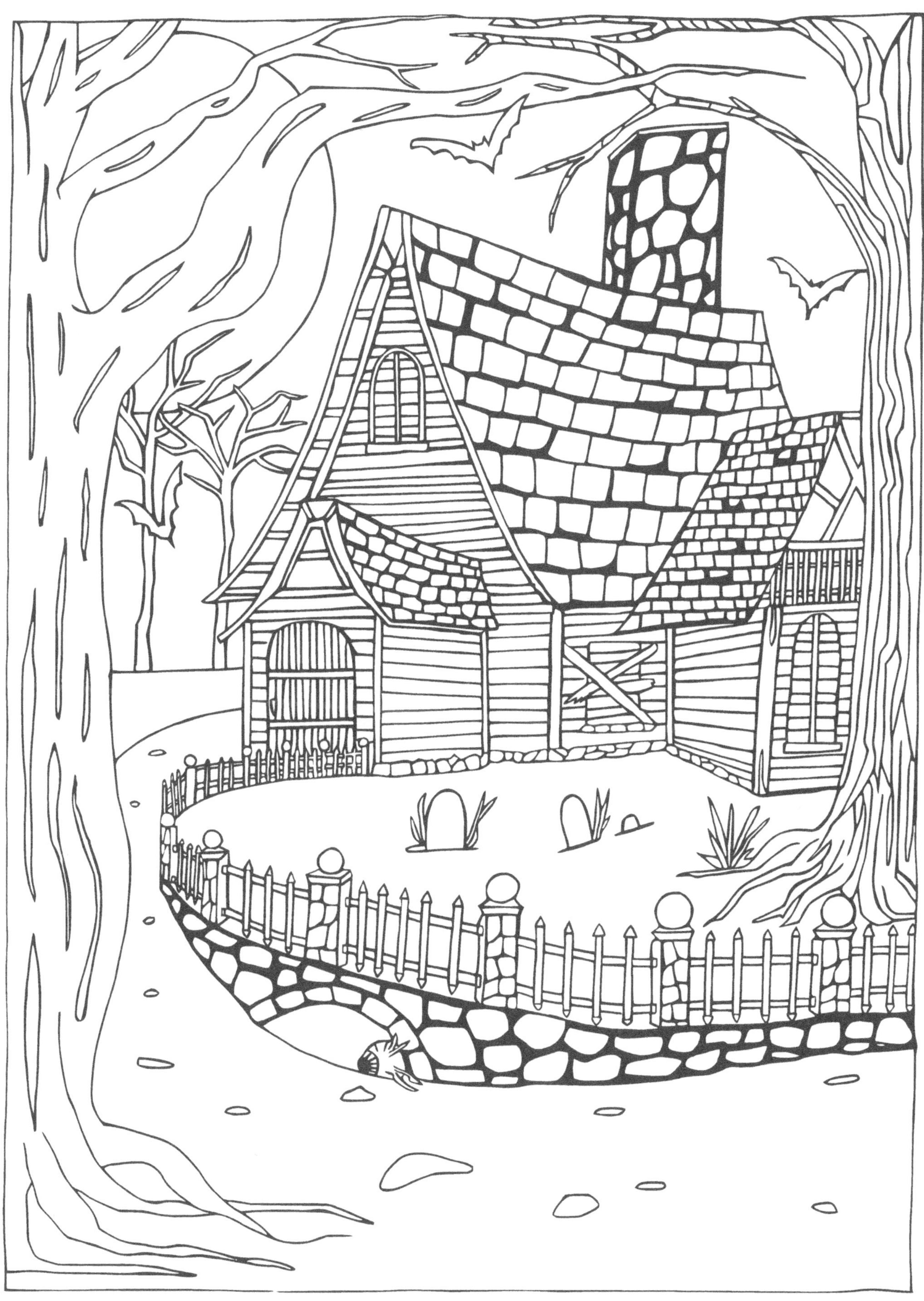

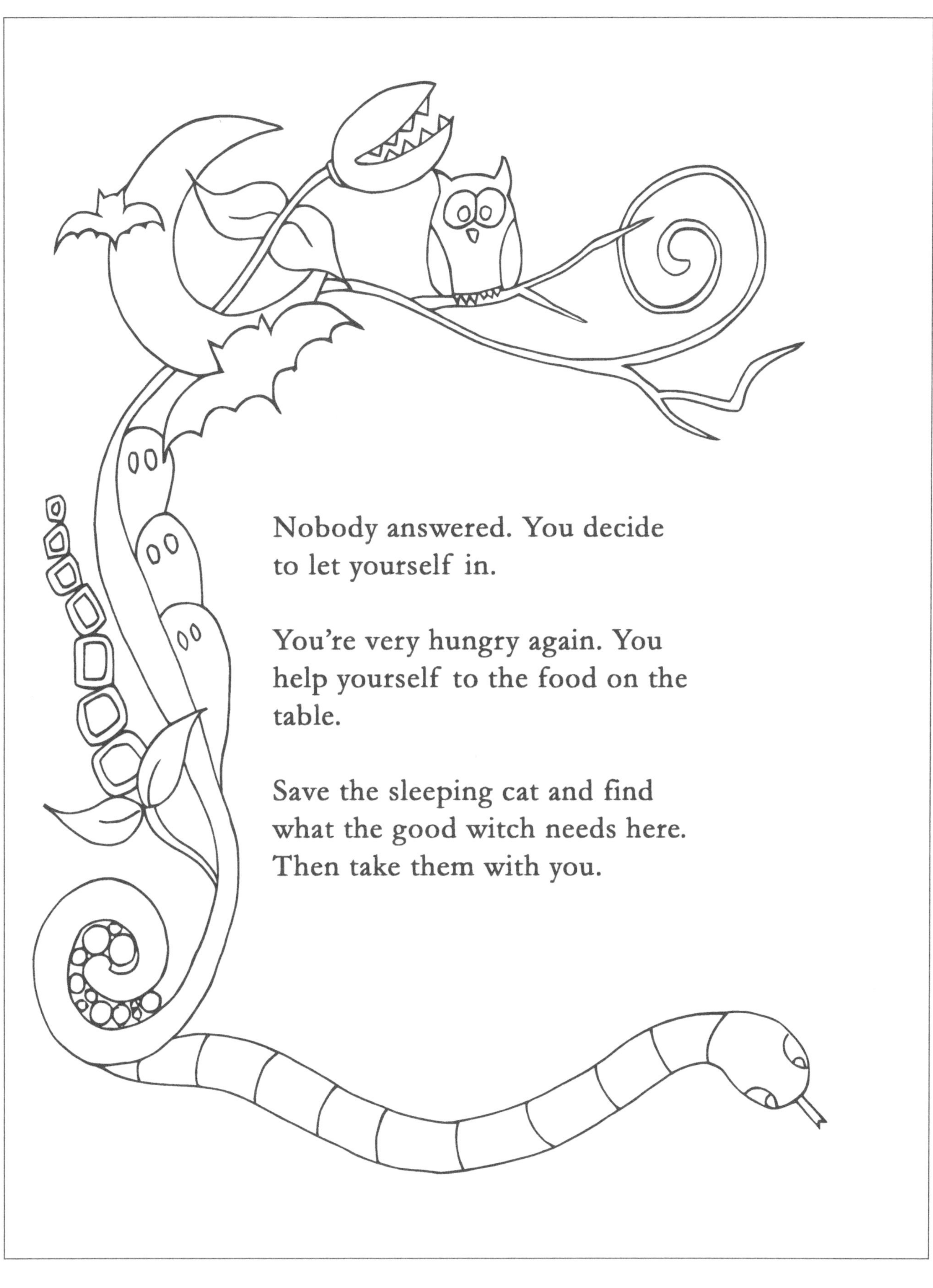

Nobody answered. You decide to let yourself in.

You're very hungry again. You help yourself to the food on the table.

Save the sleeping cat and find what the good witch needs here. Then take them with you.

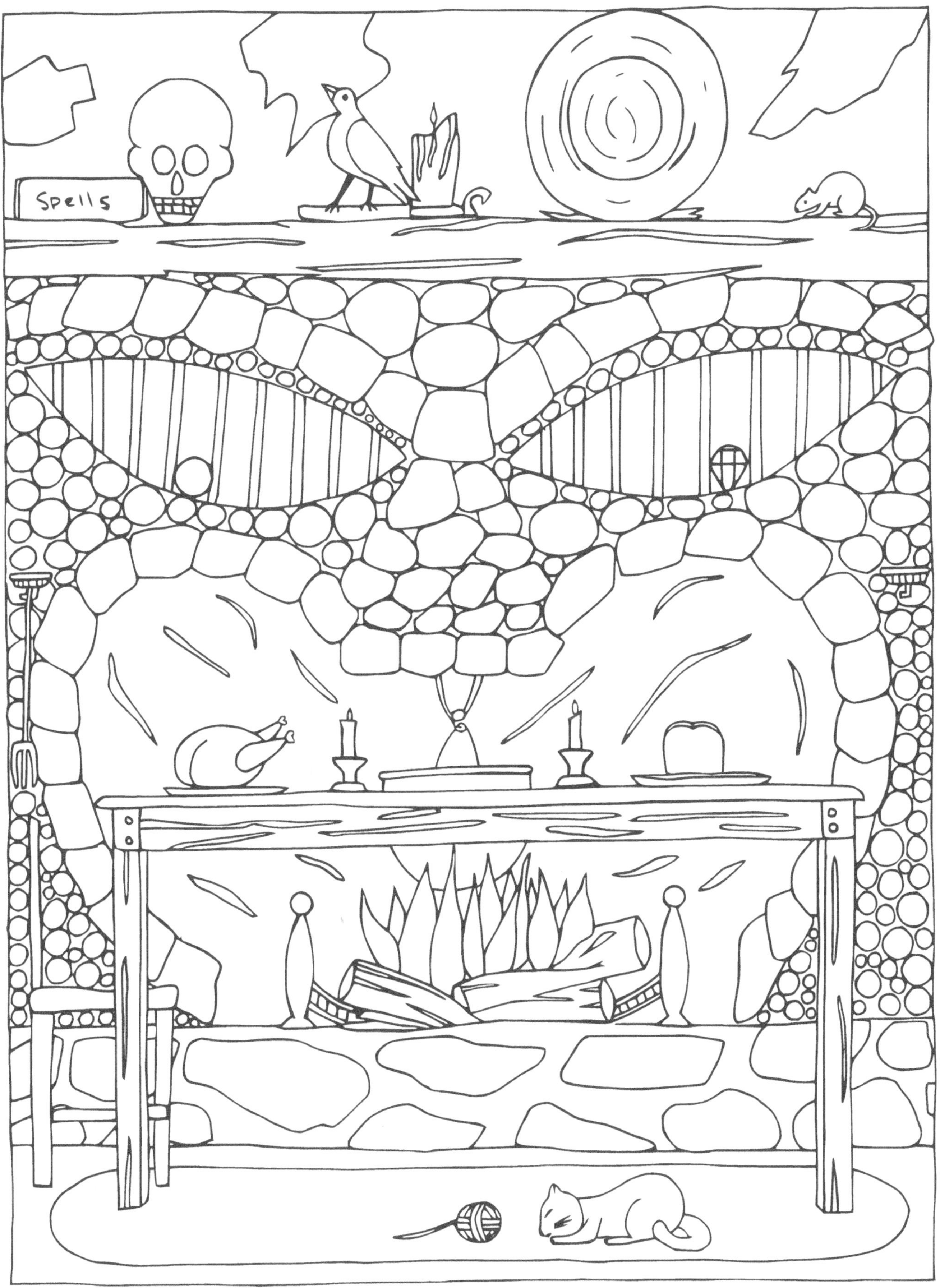
Spells

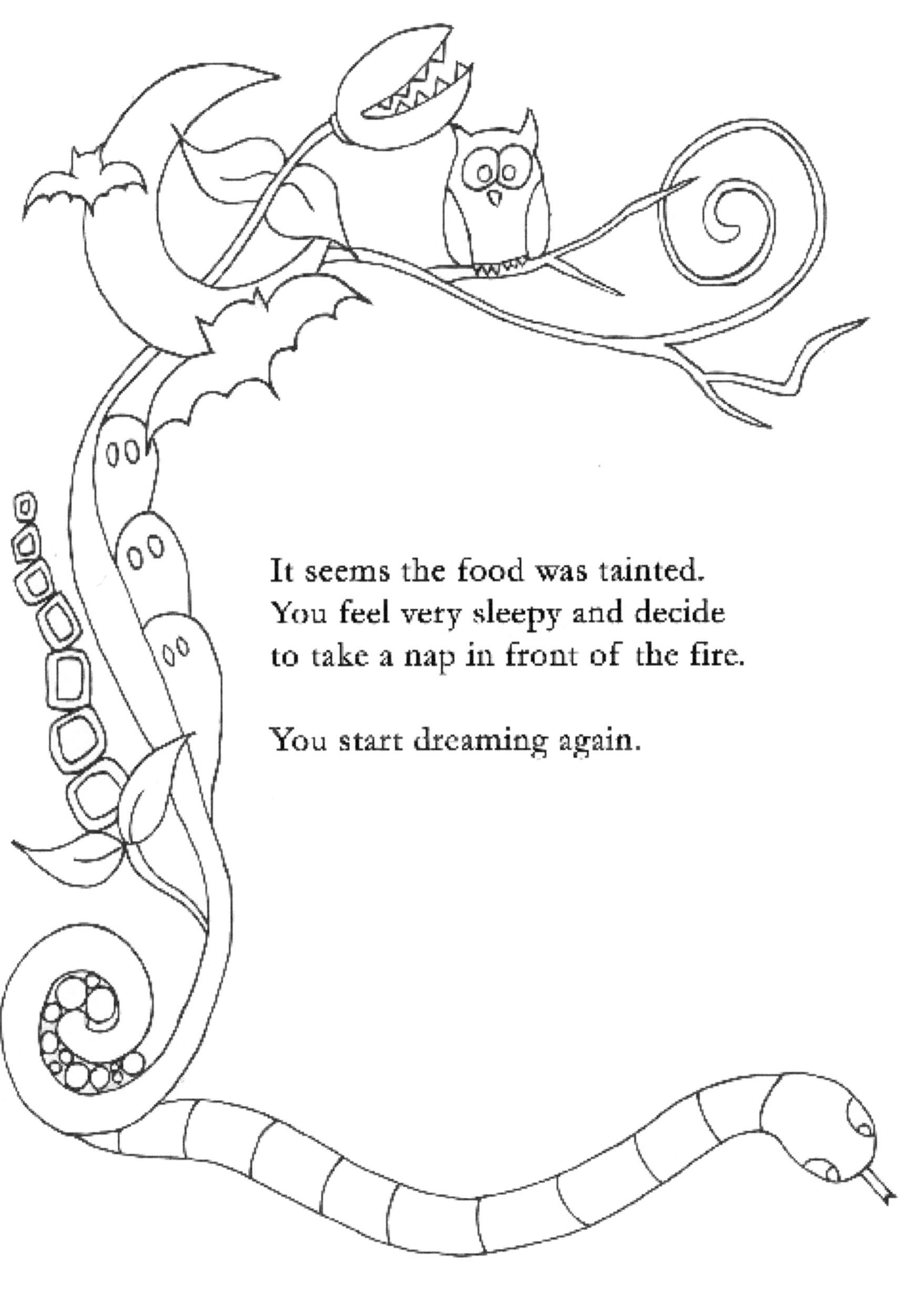

It seems the food was tainted.
You feel very sleepy and decide
to take a nap in front of the fire.

You start dreaming again.

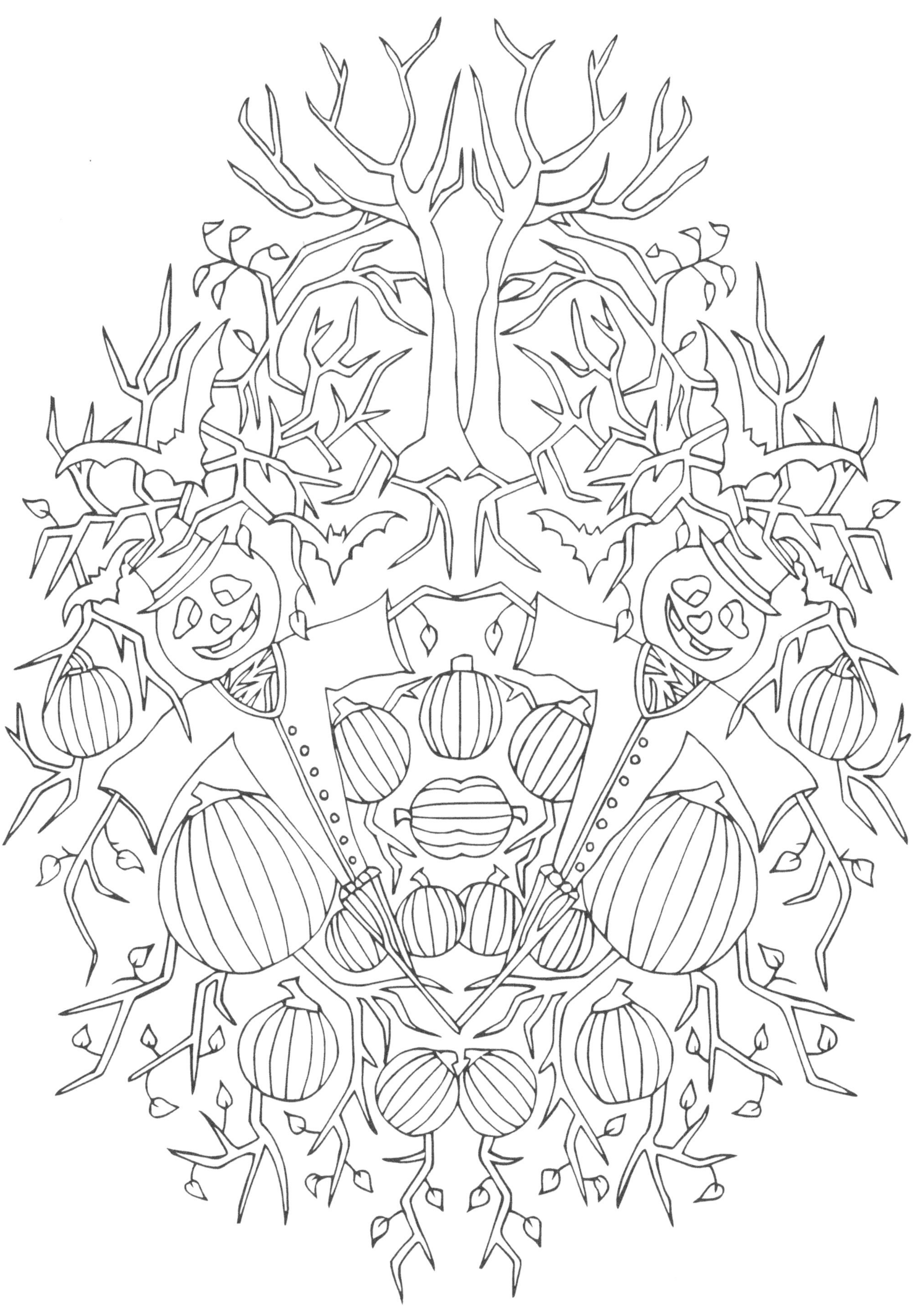

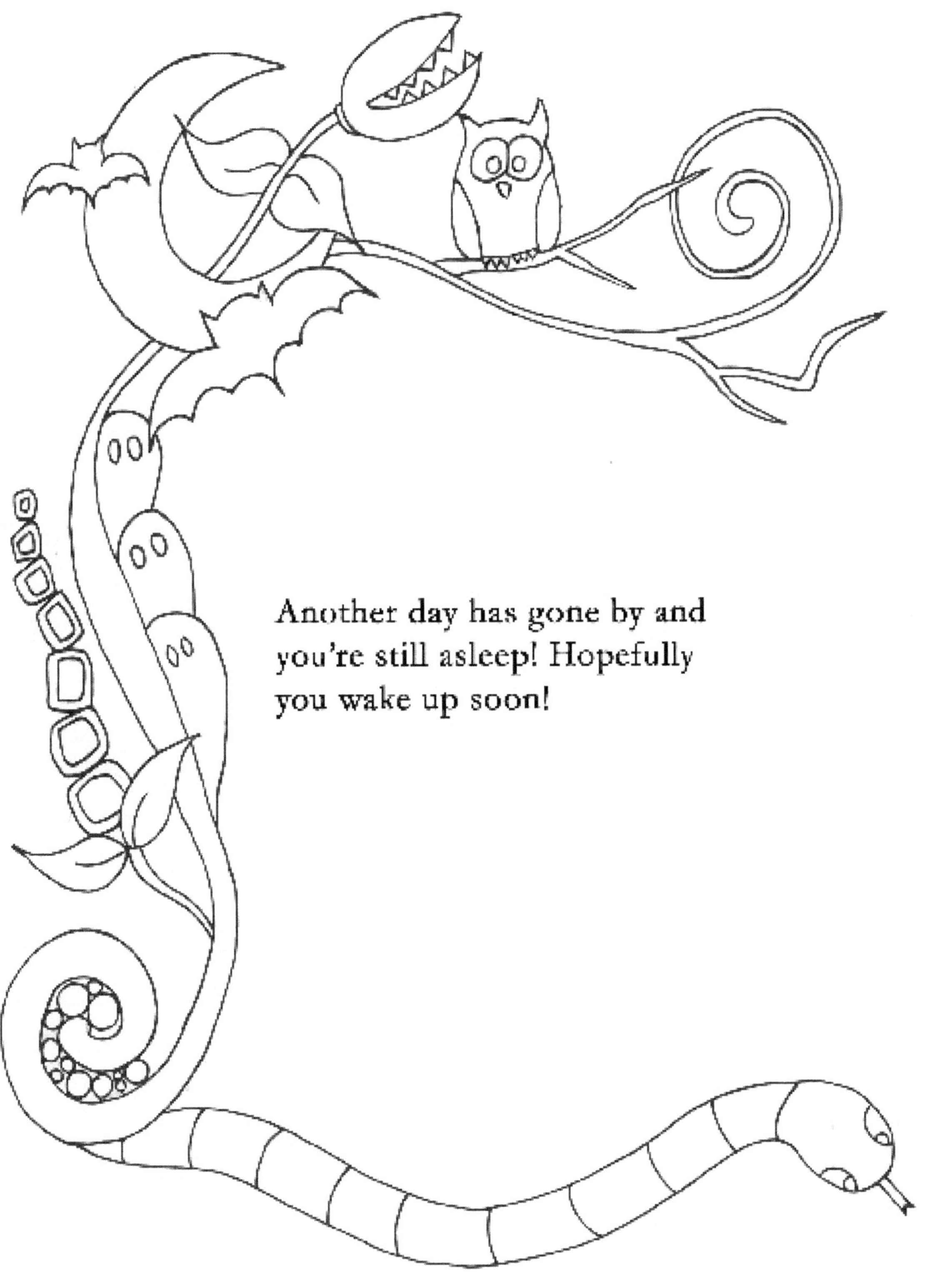

Another day has gone by and you're still asleep! Hopefully you wake up soon!

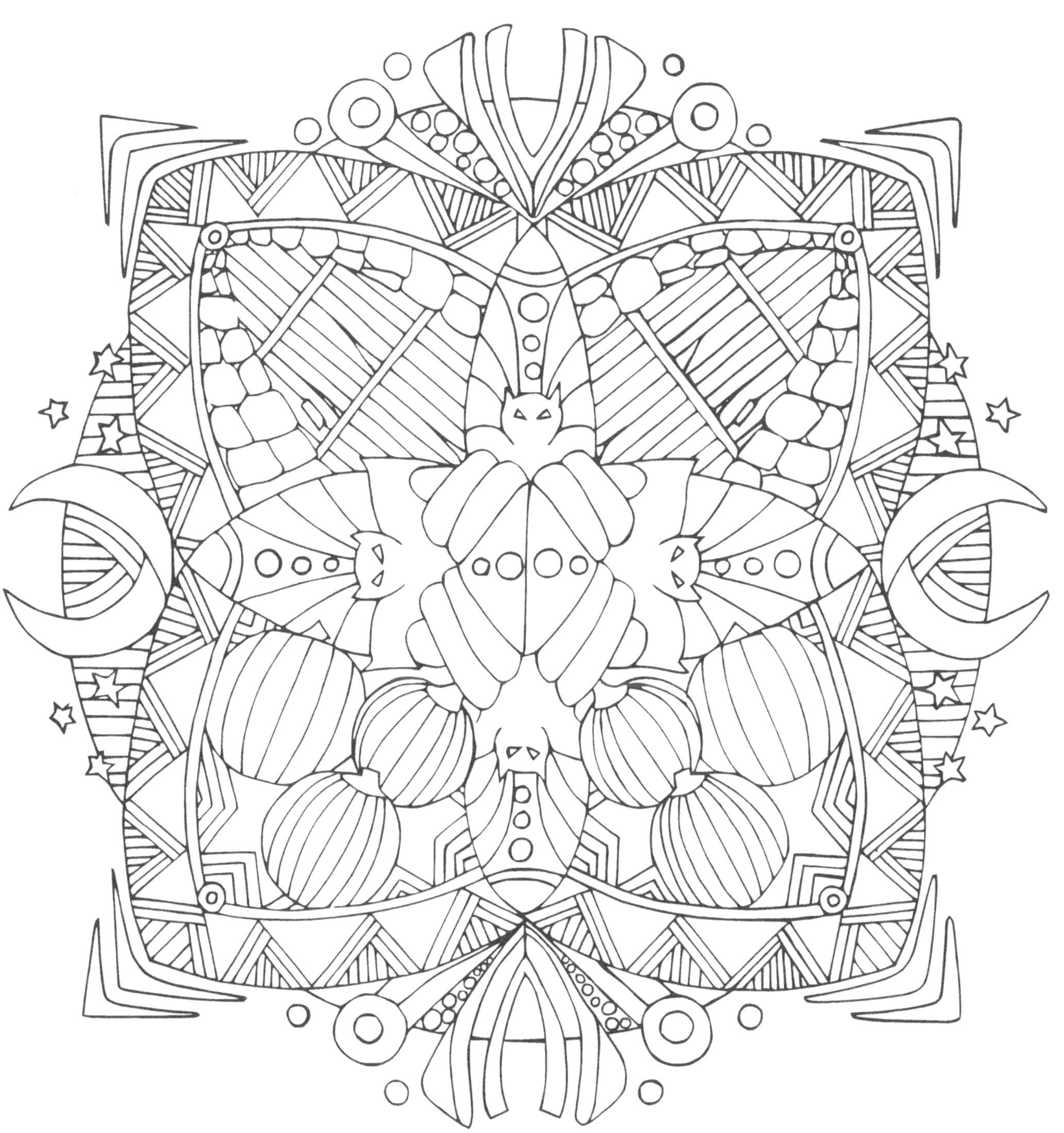

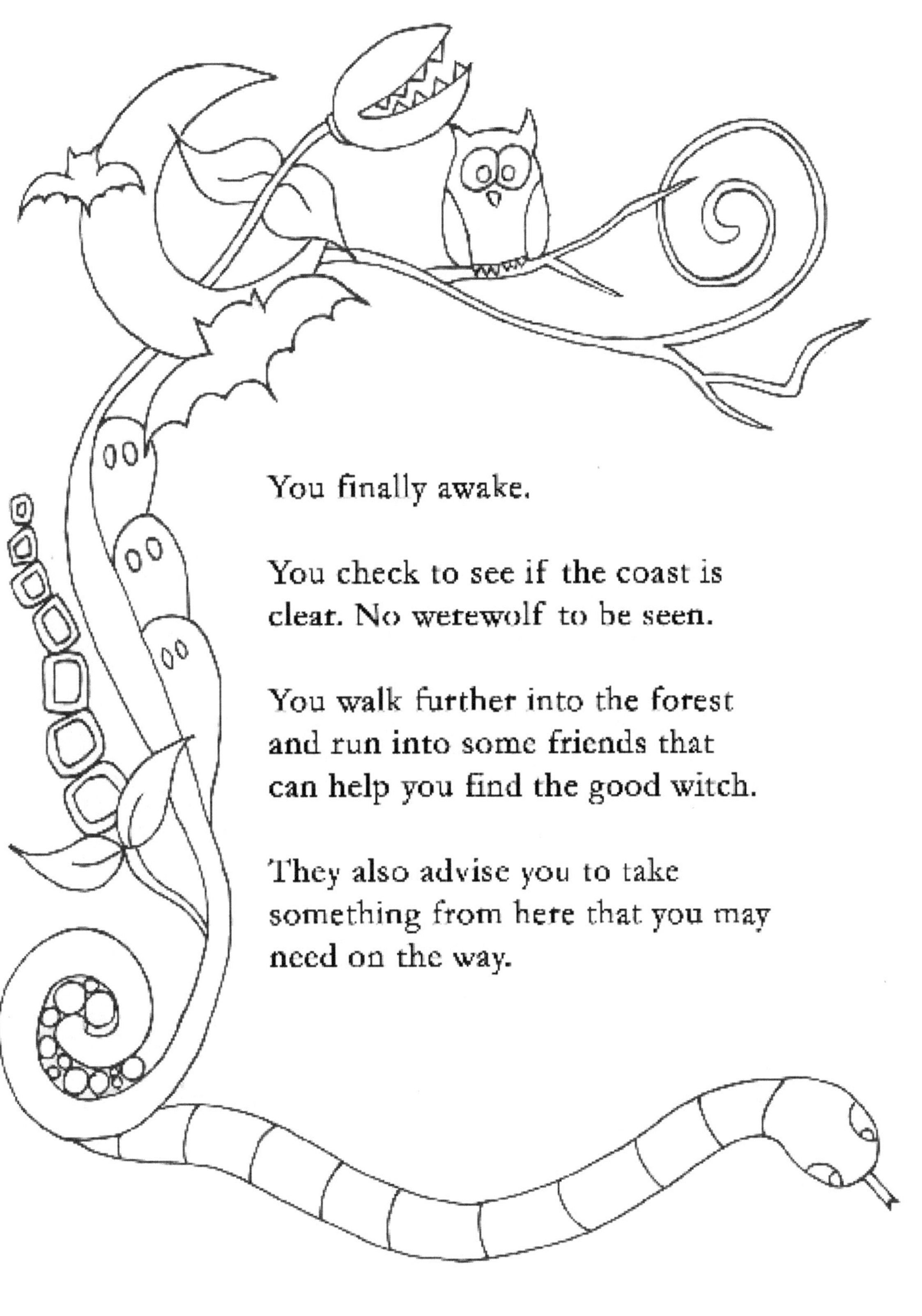

You finally awake.

You check to see if the coast is clear. No werewolf to be seen.

You walk further into the forest and run into some friends that can help you find the good witch.

They also advise you to take something from here that you may need on the way.

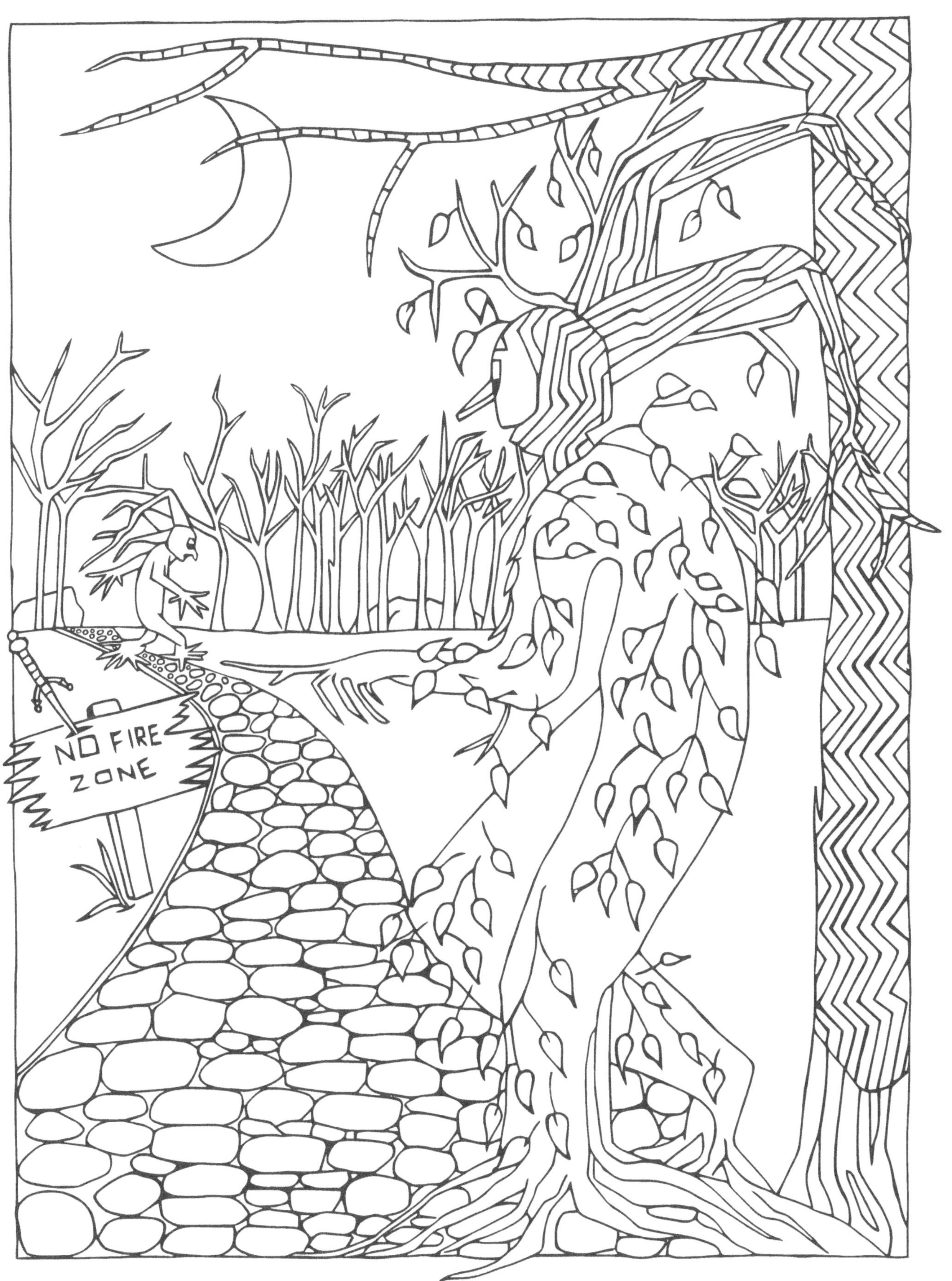
NO FIRE
ZONE

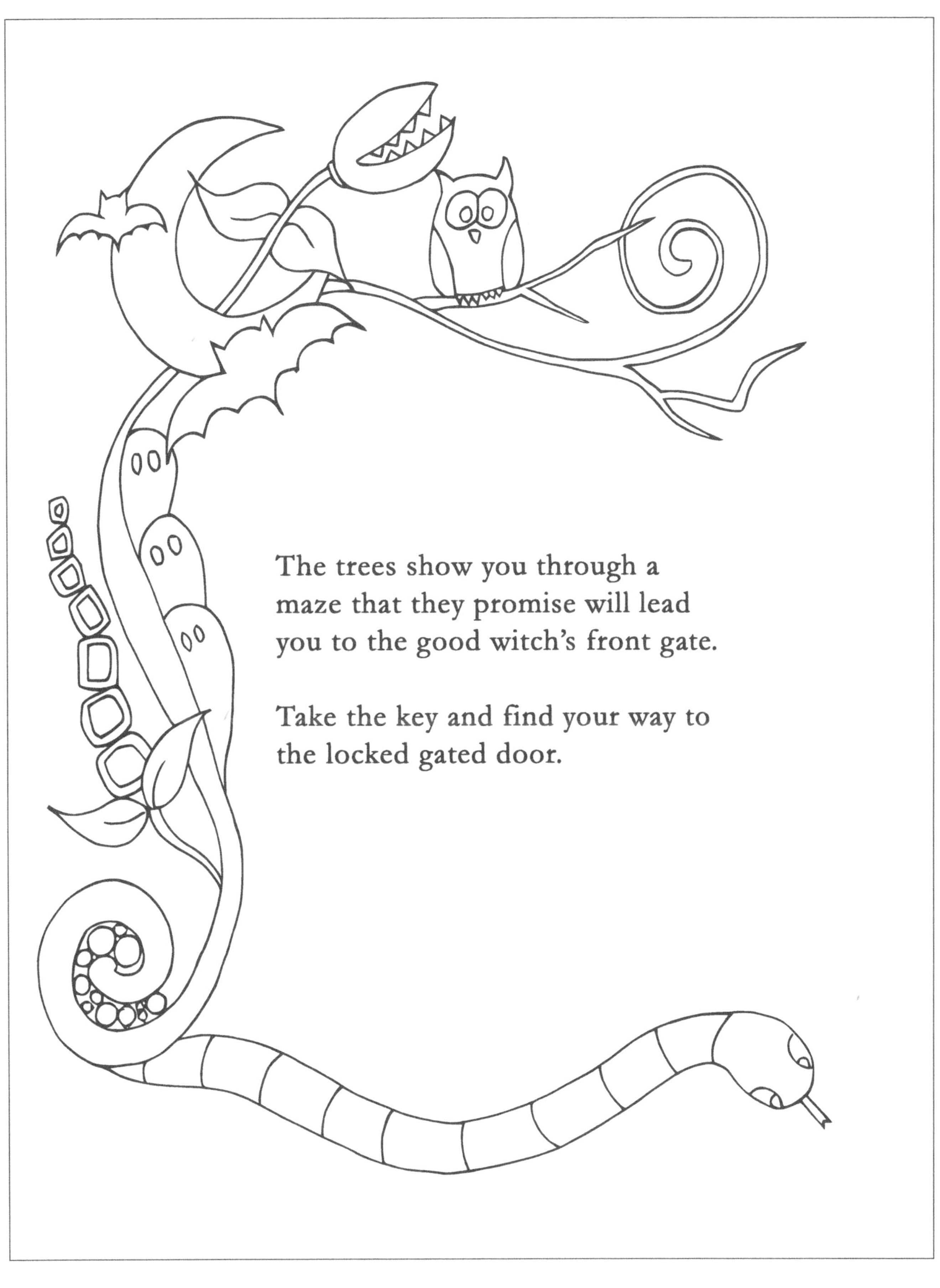

The trees show you through a maze that they promise will lead you to the good witch's front gate.

Take the key and find your way to the locked gated door.

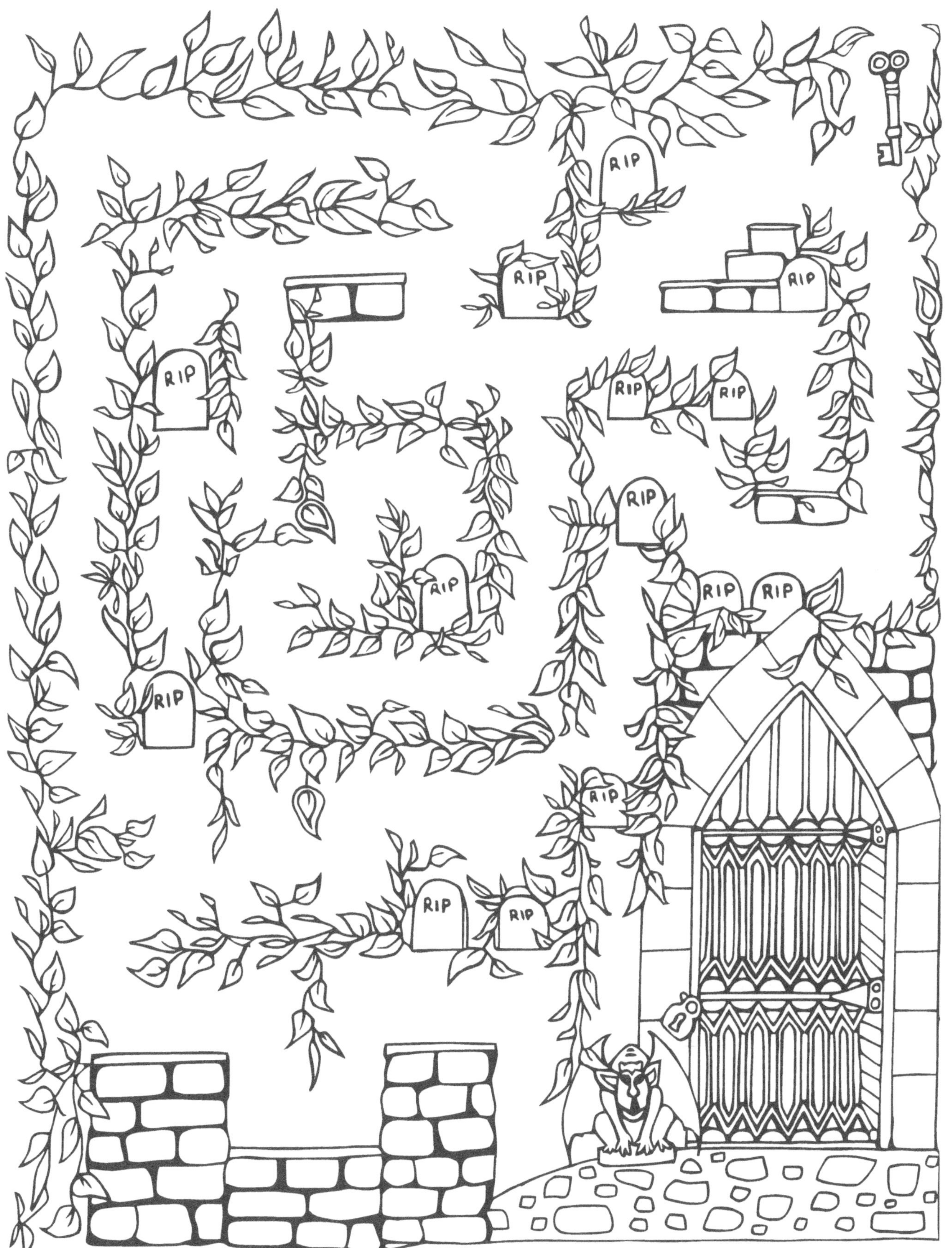
RIP
RIP
RIP
RIP
RIP
RIP
RIP
RIP
RIP
RIP
RIP
RIP
RIP
RIP

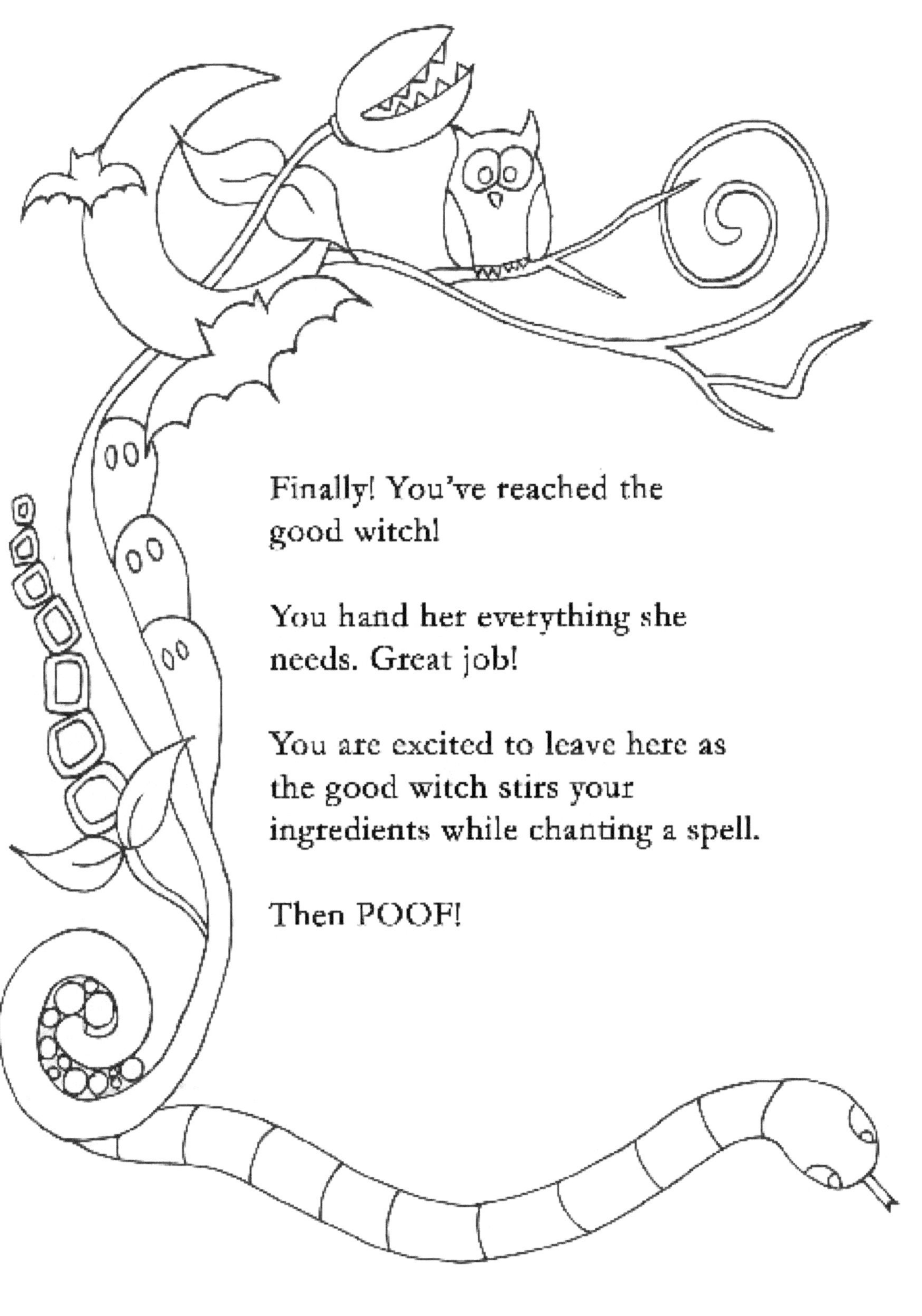

Finally! You've reached the good witch!

You hand her everything she needs. Great job!

You are excited to leave here as the good witch stirs your ingredients while chanting a spell.

Then POOF!

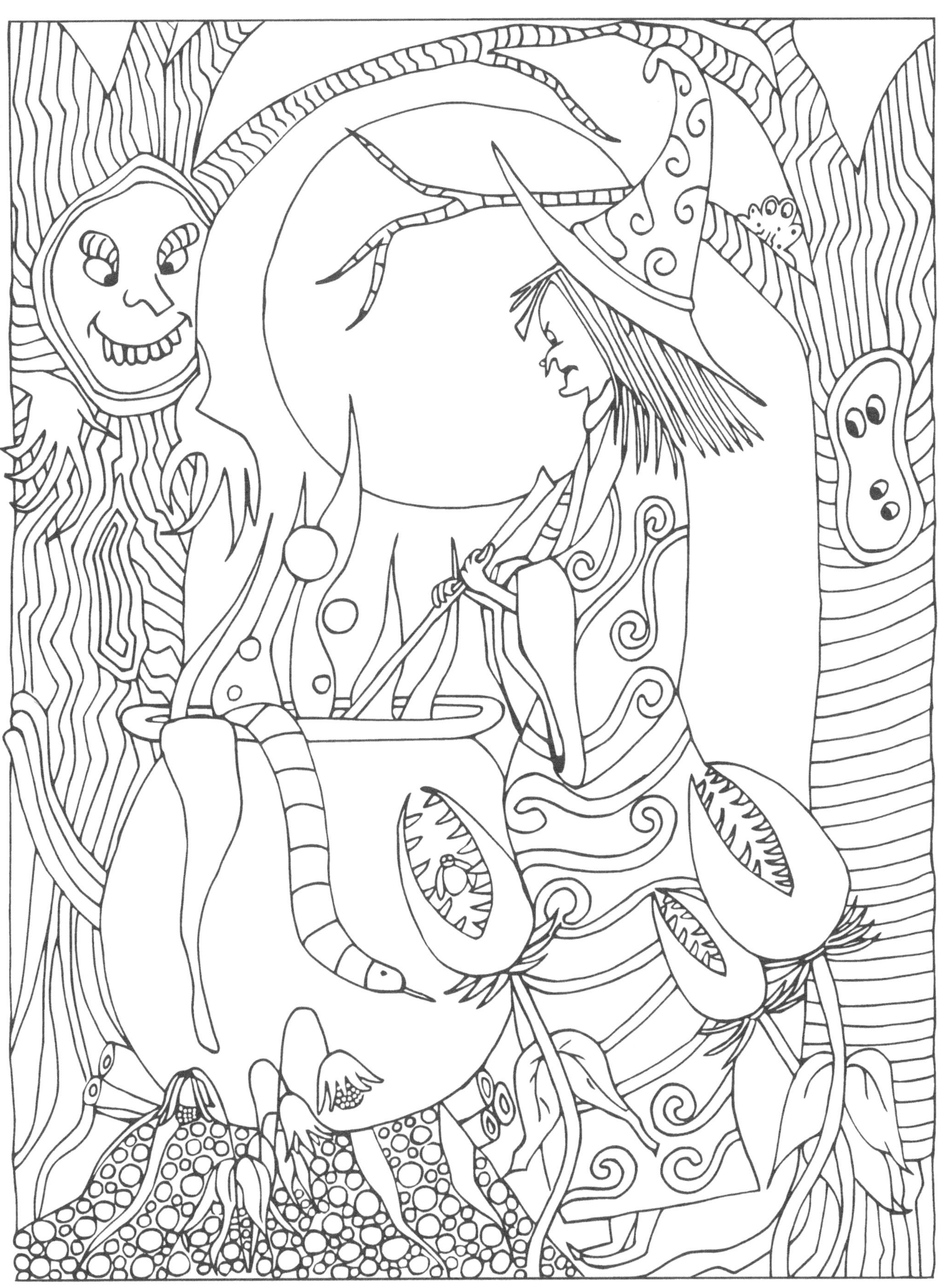

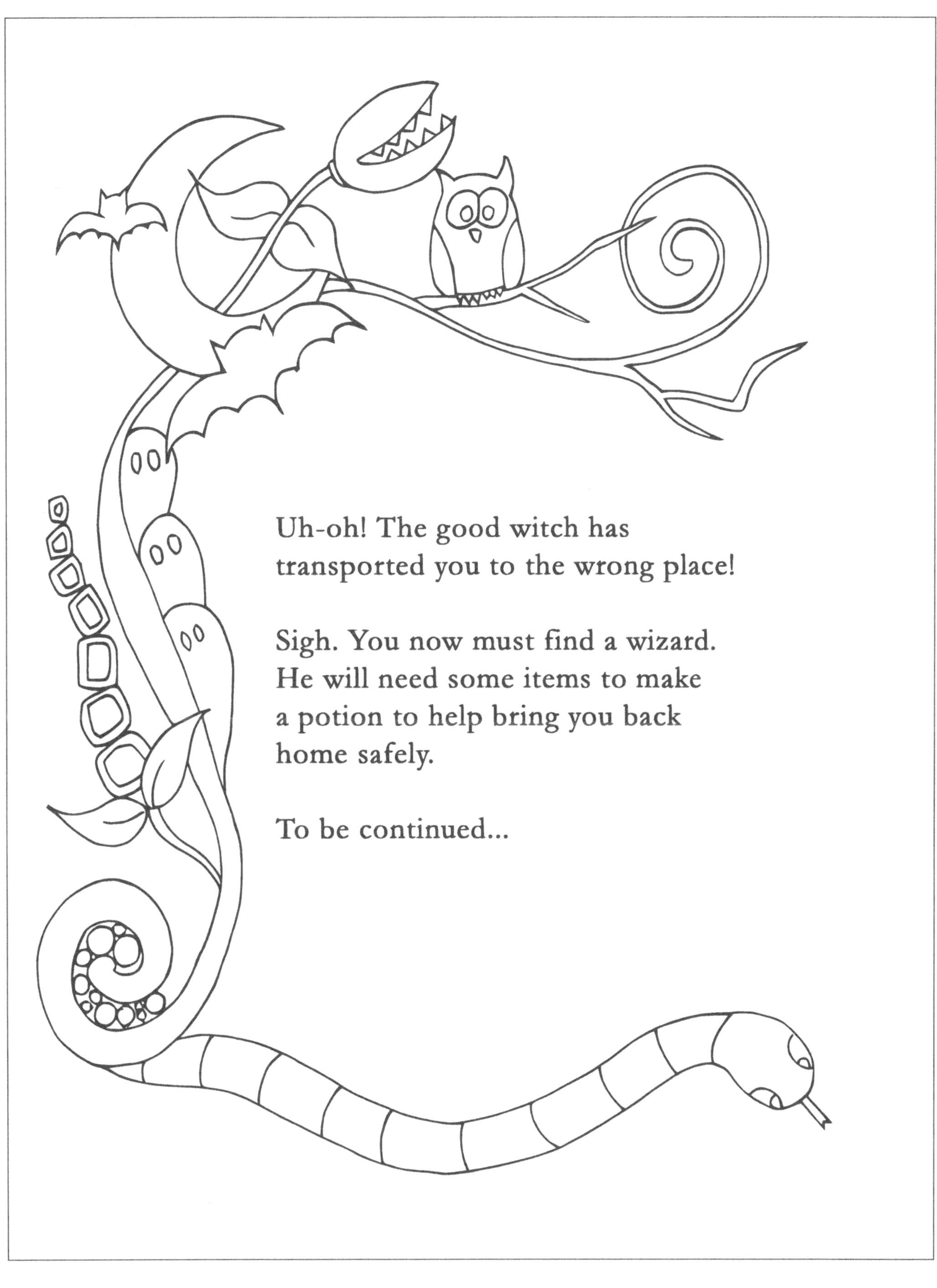

Uh-oh! The good witch has transported you to the wrong place!

Sigh. You now must find a wizard. He will need some items to make a potion to help bring you back home safely.

To be continued...

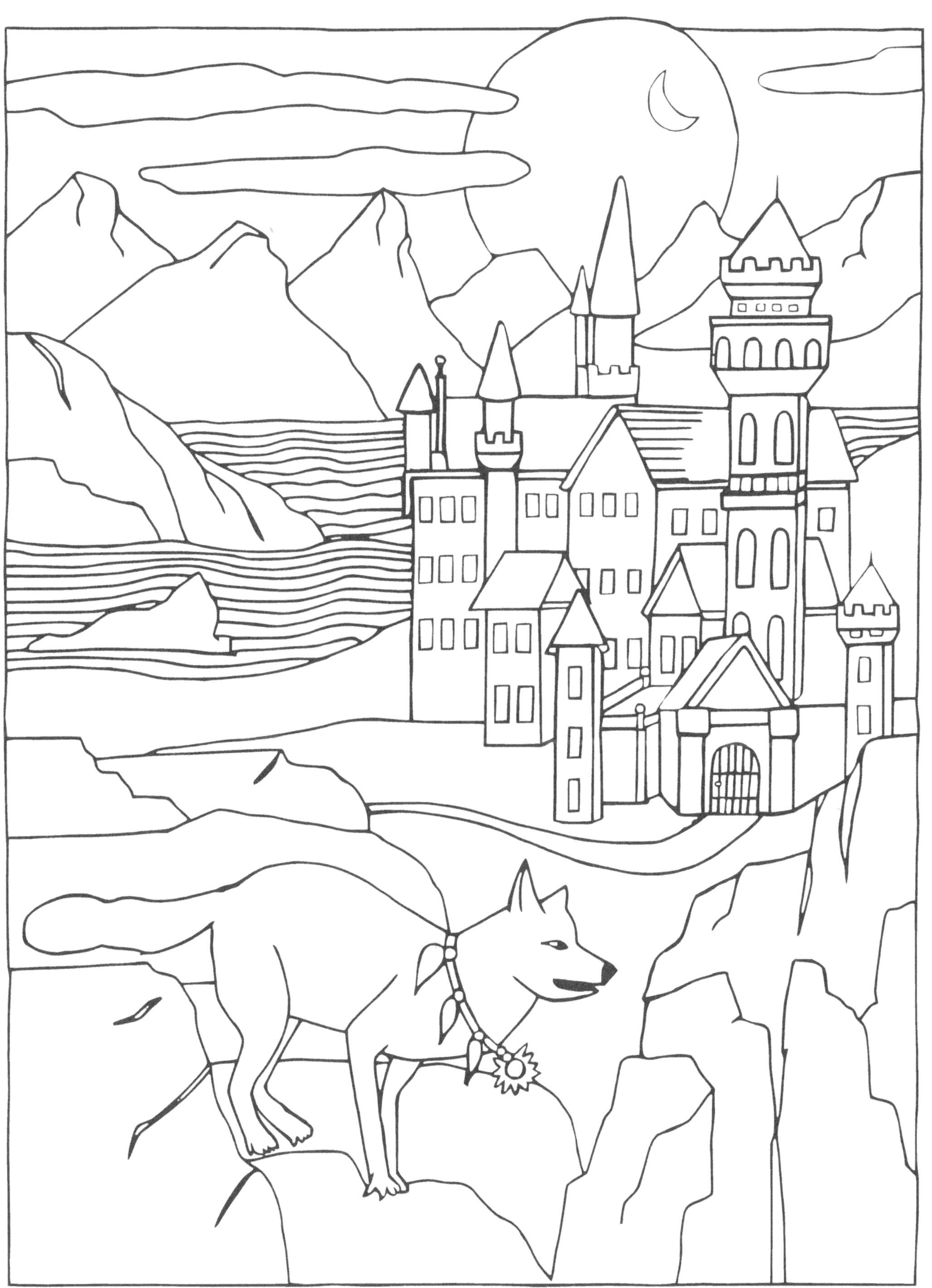

Enjoy the coloring book?

Would you like to receive my FREE monthly coloring pages?

Hi! Julia Abby Thomas here. I have the best job ever! I love creating coloring books for both experienced and beginning colorists!

When you sign-up for my FREE monthly coloring pages for experienced colorists, I will create a mix of whimsy mandalas and scenes in a variety of themes to help you de-stress at the end of the day or to spend a Saturday or Sunday morning quietly coloring in a favorite book nook.

So, sign-up at the web address below!

www.ToySurgeBooks.com/FREE-coloring-pages

or visit:
www.ToySurgeBooks.com
and look for the sign-up link.

ABOUT THE ILLUSTRATOR

Julia Abby Thomas was born in Manchester, NH. She is a former student of the Institute of Children's Literature of West Redding, CT. She has also studied at the Kimball Jenkins School of Art in Concord, NH and has been a student of award winning illustrator, Will Terry through his online Folio Academy art courses.

She has written numerous short stories and articles for various publications including her best-selling children's book series called: A Monster Stole My Shoe series.

She spends her free time watercolor painting landscapes and still life and creating coloring books for both young and experienced colorists.

Currently, she lives in Newport, NH with her fiance, Eric and her two fluffy Maine Coon cats, Maddy and Ted and the sleek short-haired Mr. Abby.

You can learn more at: www.JuliaAbbyThomas.com or by visiting her small press website at: www.ToySurgeBooks.com.

www.ingramcontent.com/pod-product-compliance
Lightning Source LLC
LaVergne TN
LVHW081407110826
845149LV00010B/1665

* 9 7 8 0 9 9 0 3 8 1 4 1 9 *